I0585540

Stories of
REMEMBERING
and
FORGETTING

Bernard Marin

**HARVARD
PUBLICATIONS**

First published in 2019 by
Harvard Publications
432 St Kilda Road
Melbourne 3004

This book is copyright. Apart from any fair
dealing for the purpose of private study,
research, criticism or review as permitted
by the *Copyright Act 1968*, no part may
be reproduced by any process without
written permission from the publisher.

Copyright © Bernard Marin 2019

The moral right of the author has been
asserted.

A catalogue record for this
book is available from the
National Library of Australia

NATIONAL
LIBRARY
OF AUSTRALIA

ISBN 9 780648 555315

Design by Skeleton Gamblers Creative

Author's note

The characters and events in these stories are a creation of the author's imagination. They are not intended to portray any person or event, and any likeness they may bear to persons or events past or present is coincidental.

Dedication

In memory of my parents, Anne and Stan Marin

Contents

The Girl on the Passport

I arrived at 26A Ogrodowa Ulica in Warsaw at two in the afternoon. It was a four-storey art deco building with the ubiquitous grey concrete render and white-framed windows of the Communist era. The street was lined with similar buildings, and leafy trees cast shadows onto parked cars and a stretch of lawn bordering the footpath. Children played on the grass and a dog barked.

I walked through a wide archway that led to a paved courtyard and turned into a narrow corridor. The apartment was at the end of the hall, and I could smell chicken soup wafting through a half-open window.

I knocked and heard a door open and close and footsteps – someone was home at least, and coming to the door.

I felt a sudden sense of unreality. It was as if all the previous years of my life had led me somehow to this moment, and all the future years of my life would depend on its outcome. I stood there for a moment, heart thudding, feeling suddenly uncertain. Then I took a deep breath and the feeling passed.

A tall, sophisticated woman opened the door, head erect, short grey hair brushed back from her face. She looked to be in her mid-seventies, with a sculpted face and a warm smile. It was a gentle face and I liked her immediately. Her eyes were wide and pale blue, not what I'd expected for a Jewish woman. She was wearing a black pleated skirt, white blouse, camel cardigan and tan silk scarf – this must be Hannah.

She looked at me and her eyes seemed to search my face for a long time. Then she smiled faintly and said in Polish, 'Yes, can I help you?'

Hesitating, I asked, 'Are you Hannah?'

She nodded cautiously. 'Who are you?'

'My name is Henry, I'm your cousin – your father's nephew.'

She looked a little uncertain. I didn't want to make her any more uncomfortable so I said, 'My father told me lots of stories about the Warsaw ghetto – about you and him.'

She breathed in sharply, and her face paled.

'Can we talk?'

She stared at me for a moment, then covered her mouth with a handkerchief and coughed, a deep, rasping cough that shook her slender body. When the coughing stopped she took off her glasses and wiped her eyes, then she put her glasses back on, and smiled at me.

'Come in,' she said, tears washing down her cheeks.

She wrapped her arm around mine and walked me down a strip of carpet that ran the length of the hall. We passed a bathroom, a telephone stand, a wall of family photos and then we were in the lounge room, where one wall was lined with floor-to-ceiling bookcases. Along the opposite wall were curtained windows that looked onto the main street, and in the corner of the room stood a grand piano. Magazines were piled on the coffee table in the centre of the room.

Hannah looked at me and smiled. 'Are you hungry?'

'No, I've just eaten.'

'Can I offer you tea?'

'Yes please.'

'Take a seat.'

I watched as she left the room, returning a few minutes later with a tray of tea things and biscuits. While she was busy with the teapot I said, 'Tell me about my father.'

She was holding a cup of tea in one hand, the bottom of the cup resting on her other palm. She hesitated, then put the cup on the low table, looked at me and was silent for so long I thought she might not speak at all. She filled her own cup and, putting a cube of sugar between her teeth, she sipped slowly, letting the tea soak through the sugar. I could see she was collecting her thoughts, perhaps wondering where to begin. 'What can I say?' Her soft voice broke, and the last word came out husky.

'Tell me about the Warsaw ghetto.'

Hannah sat for a long time, looking first at me, then out the window, then back to me. I could see she was nervous.

'How did you and Dad get separated?'

She lifted her head to look at me and I saw her eyes were sad.

Later, when she finished speaking, she seemed to withdraw into herself. I didn't know what to say. I forced a smile. Hannah seemed tired and her eyes were misty. She picked up her cup, then put it down again. Finally she looked at her watch and said, 'It's getting late.'

'Can we continue tomorrow?'

'Of course,' she said. 'Thank you for coming to see me.' Her voice trembled.

Three months earlier I could never have imagined I would be sitting in a Warsaw apartment with a cousin I had never known, or that she would have such a story to tell.

'So, what's planned for LA?' I said. It was winter, 2000, and we'd all recovered from our fear of flying when no planes fell from the sky on New Year's day, despite apocalyptic warnings in the lead-up to the new millennium.

Judy put her finger to her lips, indicating the kids, who were slumped in their seats, sound asleep.

'Disneyland, Universal Studios, the Getty Centre and the Museum of Tolerance.'

I looked at her. 'You're joking. The Museum of Tolerance?'

'It's one of the best Holocaust museums in the world.'

'It's the last place I want to spend my holidays,' I said.

'Everybody says it's a must.'

I considered this for a moment. 'But this is meant to be fun,' I said, hearing the plaintive note in my voice.

Judy just looked at me. I forced myself to meet her gaze. 'And the kids, will they be interested?'

'They need to understand their heritage, what it means to be Jewish,' Judy said.

'That's why you insisted we send them to a Jewish school,' I said. 'You chose Mount Scopus, not me, remember. It does a good job with the Holocaust.'

'Fine,' she said. 'Don't come.'

Silence. It seemed the subject was closed. This was the point at which I usually gave in, but instead I turned to the window and shut my eyes. The voices of the kids in the seats behind grated and the thought of having to spend a day at the Museum of Tolerance irritated me. Clearly I wasn't going to be able to sleep, at least not for a while. And it wasn't that I didn't want to know about the Holocaust, it was that I already knew too much.

As kids, my sister and I had spent many bedtime hours with Mum talking about the Holocaust. Most children listened to Snugglepot and Cuddlepie at bedtime, but not us. I lost count of the number of times Mum said, 'You were named after your father's brother – he was a gifted pianist. We lost him at Treblinka, with so many others.'

I remembered my parents' response when, at eighteen, I told them I didn't want to go to university, I wanted to become a musician. Mum was standing at the sink with her back to me and Dad was sitting at the table in his pyjamas. 'You're not leaving school,' he said. 'Fine, go to the conservatorium and study real music, but you're not going to throw away your life.'

I stared at my toast.

'When we came to Australia we had nothing. The Nazis deprived me of an education but I worked hard and made something of myself just so we could be financially secure. Education is important. Lawyers, doctors, earn good money. How much money do you think you'll get playing the guitar?' he demanded.

I remember leaving the kitchen, wanting to run away from the house and its oppressive atmosphere of guilt and ghosts. It seemed that every aspect of my past, and now my future, was contaminated by the Holocaust.

It was drizzling lightly when we arrived at the Museum of Tolerance. In the end I had decided to come out of respect for those who had died and those who had survived the camps. I also wanted to avoid having to justify my absence to my children, which might have opened up the subject of my childhood and my family. You could say I took the path of least resistance.

The brown building was unobtrusive. Five leafy trees in planter boxes stood in front of what looked like stepped shipping containers. Inside it was stark, sterile and cold and the visitors' faces were solemn.

After we'd left our coats and bags, I turned to Judy and said, 'These old guides remind me of my father.'

'I understand this is hard for you, Henry, but think of the children,' Judy said.

'There is plenty of time for them to learn about such horrors; does it have to be now?'

Judy ignored me.

We were ushered downstairs to an open auditorium where we were subjected to an orientation. Our guide rattled out a stream of statistics and droned on about the themes of the museum; he described the Holocaust as 'the ultimate example of man's inhumanity to man'.

The briefing over, we were set free. Walking past the section on the Cambodian atrocities and Armenian genocide, we arrived at the Holocaust section. As we entered, each of us received a photo passport; mine belonged to a young girl, who looked to be about thirteen years old, with dark eyes and olive skin. According to the brief description on the card, she was born in Warsaw, like my father.

'Another horrible Holocaust story. I can't stand it,' I muttered and put the passport in my pocket.

Next, we were herded together and a timed tour moved us to an exhibit titled, 'The Rise and Fall of the Third Reich'. We stood in front of a re-creation of a 1930s Berlin café where people were discussing Hitler's rise to power and the Nazi takeover of Germany. I imagined the couple at the table were my paternal grandparents. As if reading my mind, my son Adam said to me, 'Were your parents from Germany or Poland, Dad?'

'Warsaw, but my mother escaped to Russia – that's how she survived.'

'And your father?' my daughter asked.

'He wasn't so lucky, Romy.'

'Did you know your grandparents?' Adam asked.

'No,' I said. 'And I'm glad I didn't.'

'Why?' he asked, gazing up at me, his face registering his disapproval.

'My father was so enmeshed in the past – never able to move beyond the Holocaust – I think he got most of his meshugas from his parents, although he endured a lot.'

'But it wasn't their fault,' Adam said.

'I know it wasn't deliberate, but growing up with that was hard,' I said. 'My dad had enough problems of his own without having to carry his parents' problems as well.'

'Can you tell us a bit about them?' Romy asked.

'Well, briefly, my paternal grandfather was a merchant. They were a well-to-do family who lived in the part of Warsaw that later became the Jewish ghetto.'

'Why didn't they leave before the war?' Romy asked.

I sighed. 'I don't know. Maybe they thought their connections would protect them or maybe they didn't realise how bad it would get. Who could have known what lay ahead …?'

Romy leaned forward and nodded, encouraging me to continue.

'But had they left, my life would have been very different – much happier – and so would their life, and my father's. But who knew?'

Romy looked at me and frowned. Turning away, I said to Judy. 'I need a coffee – I'll see you at the next exhibit.'

'Are you all right?'

'I'll be fine,' I snapped.

'Maybe a double scotch?'

I forced a smile and turned towards the café.

As I sat drinking my coffee, I remembered one Shabbos when I was about fifteen. At the table that evening Dad had been subdued. He kept staring at me throughout the meal, looking as if he was on the verge of tears. At one point, after a long silence, he said, 'If there was a God he would have saved those six million Jews.'

Before I went to sleep that night I asked my mother, 'What was the matter with Dad at dinner?'

'Today is the anniversary of his brother's disappearance.'

'Oh, that's really sad,' I said.

'Yes,' she replied.

A waiter came and collected my empty coffee cup, pulling me back to the present. I realised I needed to return to my family.

I found them in the information room where visitors were inserting their passports into a computer to receive an update on their person's life. Judy turned and looked at me. 'Better now?' she said.

I shrugged.

The kids queued to put their passports into the computer, but I held back, not wanting to know what had happened to the girl whose life story was in my pocket.

'Did you get your printout, Dad?' Romy asked.

Once again, I decided that it was easier to go along with them than to protest and draw attention to myself. With a sigh, I inserted my photo passport into the computer and received a printout of the child's experiences.

I learned she had been forced into the Warsaw ghetto with her grandmother along with 400,000 other Jews. The printout explained that the girl had come from an affluent family, but in the ghetto she shared a room with ten others, was often hungry and could not sleep at night.

Reading her story reminded me of Hannah, my father's niece. I had heard her story many times during my childhood. Hannah's parents had left Warsaw for Vilna on a business trip, just before the German offensive, and then couldn't return. She was left in the safekeeping of my father. The two of them escaped the deportations and ended up in the Warsaw ghetto, where my father found work as a tailor. During the day Hannah was free to clamber through the tunnels that connected the ghetto with the 'Aryan' side to scavenge for food.

One day, when my father returned from work, Hannah was not waiting for him. A few people said they had seen her disappear through the gates of the ghetto. My father told me he made many attempts to get to the Polish side to find her, but it was impossible. He eventually gave up hope for his niece, convinced she had been shot by the Nazis. Soon after, my father was relocated to Majdanek, a death camp, where he was used as slave labour. He eventually ended up in Auschwitz.

Judy and the kids had followed the guide to an interactive exhibit and were listening to a survivor's recorded testimony. I tuned out and thought again of my father. When I buried him fifteen years ago, I had made a conscious decision to close the door on the oppressiveness of my family's past and my own childhood. But now, in this museum, it was all rushing back. I felt that familiar heaviness in my chest, as if I were being suffocated.

I started walking towards the café to escape from it all, but I could not forget the face of my young girl and my pace slowed. It felt disrespectful not to honour her experience, not to understand her story. I took out her passport and continued reading about her life.

Like Dad and Hannah, she had fought in the Warsaw ghetto uprising of April 1943. Surprised, I looked again at her photograph: she did not seem old enough. But I remembered my father telling me that most of the Jewish soldiers of the uprising had been little more than children, and their commander, Mordechai Anielewicz, was in his early twenties when the insurrection took place. I had always imagined my father's niece as daring, brave and full of hope – just like the girl on the passport. Having made the connection between her and Hannah, I felt compelled to continue through the exhibits.

As I followed her story, I learned that she had not survived the war. Everyone assumed that she had perished during the fighting in the ghetto uprising; whatever the case, she was never seen again.

We followed our guide to the Hall of Testimony where we witnessed the stories of many survivors. It was an empty, cold room and the sprinklers on the ceiling reminded me of the gas chambers. I shuddered at the thought of my family, my people, moments before their death – all my father's uncles, aunts and their children – who were sent to Treblinka. I had thought that hearing countless stories about the Holocaust as a kid had inured me to its horrors.

From the Hall of Testimony we moved on to our next stop: a re-creation of the death camp of Auschwitz. The exhibit was deliberately dirty, dark and surrounded with barbed wire. An eerie silence had fallen on the people looking at it.

As we entered the exhibit we were confronted with two lanes – one for the small number of people deemed able to work and the other for the majority of victims: women, children and the elderly who were sent to the gas chambers on arrival. In many cases, the entire transport was sent to their immediate death.

I pictured my father there, for this is where he had ended up. He saw crowds of people driven and whipped through the camp to the gas chambers.

A plaque on the wall described the work of the Sonderkommando: a group of Jewish men who were forced to calm the people on arrival, selecting those for the gas chambers, sorting the victims' possessions and later removing corpses. Very few of these men survived because they were witnesses to the genocide, but those who did survive lived with the guilt of having sent fellow Jews to their deaths. And many survivors accused them of being complicit with the Nazis.

As I stood there looking at the exhibit, I started to appreciate, really for the first time, the extent of my father's torment. He had been a member of the Sonderkommando. He had survived but was plagued with survivor guilt.

A memory suddenly came to me: I was in Acland Street with Dad on a Sunday morning when a group of men spat at us as we walked past. 'Shame on you,' they hissed. My father refused to talk about the incident, and would not explain why it had happened.

I looked across at Adam who was clearly struggling to comprehend the incomprehensible. I thought of my dead father who had tried to make me understand. He had suffered and I had suffered because of his suffering. He was unable to show love or compassion or empathy. After he had lost everyone and found himself alone, he seemed afraid to allow himself to love again. I wondered whether Hannah's survival would have made things different for him.

We left the Holocaust exhibition, but Judy and the children were keen to see other parts of the museum. It was too much for me: I needed time to compose myself, to free myself from the unsought recollections of my father and the memories of my childhood.

I noticed feedback cards near the door so I sat down to complete one. In the space provided for additional comments, I felt compelled to write something of my father's story. I also described how the young girl's passport had affected me, how she had reminded me of my cousin, Hannah.

Cousin: I realised that I had used the word for the first time. Yes, she was my cousin.

We left the museum and continued our holiday, but my father's ghost haunted me and I could not stop thinking about him. I regretted allowing the years to drift by; I regretted how seldom we had spoken, how little we'd shared of ourselves; I regretted not taking the time to pick up the phone or visit.

Three months after our return, I received a letter from the director of the museum. Initially I mistook it for an advertising brochure and was about to toss it in the bin when I saw 'Private and Confidential' marked in red on the envelope.

One of the museum researchers had read my family story and believed she had some information about a close relative. The woman was now in her seventies and had been raised in Poland as a Christian after the war. She had made contact with Jewish organisations in Israel and America in the hope of discovering information about her family, who had died during the Holocaust. The researcher believed that this woman was my cousin.

I was stunned. My mind raced with a million questions as I picked up the phone to call the museum. I could not turn my back on this. Here was the link to my father's world; I was sure this was Hannah. I needed to know more, to make contact, to hear about her, and to see her. She would tell me what had happened. I would discover it on my father's behalf.

Two days later I was on a plane to Poland.

'Good morning,' I said as Hannah opened the door.

She looked thin and worn, her eyes red in her pale face. She looked as if she hadn't slept all night. 'Come in,' she said in a low voice, smiling faintly.

I followed her down the hall, resumed my seat from the previous day and watched her pour tea. After passing a cup to me she filled her own cup and, took a sugar cube. Then she put the cup down and nodded as if to say, let's start.

'Thank you for taking the time to see me,' I said.

'You're family, how could I not?'

'How did you and Dad get separated?' I hadn't meant to blurt out such a question. There was a long moment of silence. When she finally spoke, her voice was warm.

'I'll never forget that day. It was the eve of Passover – 19 April 1943. I remember it was around four in the afternoon when I tried to get back into the ghetto. But the uprising had started and it was impossible to get past the SS. I was forced to stay on the Aryan side, so I went to see friends of my parents for help and luckily they were willing to look after me. I spent the rest of the war hiding in their cellar.'

Hannah lifted her head and looked at me for a long moment. She seemed to be searching for something she had been missing for a long time.

'My life under the occupation and after the war was very hard. From the moment I lost my parents my path was strewn with tears.'

She looked down at the floor as she spoke and her voice was seared with pain.

'I was left alone after the war, not equipped for life, helpless, without any means. I worked in various offices – I knew Russian and French well …'

She spoke quietly now, as if all this were routine.

'Shortly after the war, there were more pogroms and Jews started leaving Poland – all heading towards Israel. I was so alone I was frightened – I was in a terrible situation.'

I sat waiting as her sad eyes fixed on mine.

'I could not remain in Poland but I had no way out. It was a time when single women were getting married just to escape this second hell. After long deliberations and against my better judgement, I also decided to take this step, in order to survive.'

I felt my throat constricting. Even after the war this woman had suffered. She finished her tea and said, almost as if she was talking to herself, 'Sometimes I get the feeling we're nothing more than ants to be trodden on.' She no longer seemed to see me.

'I left for Israel – foreign country, strange people, heavy climate – and there I fell into another misery. The man I married turned out to be evil and despotic, he treated me badly. Once more I walked on a tear-strewn path. In those days I was remembering my lost family, whose memory will always stay with me, and those people dear to them, and therefore dear to me.'

I could not hold back the tears. When Hannah spoke next her voice was low and subdued. 'At the moment when there seems to be no meaning in life, one needs to find a new meaning. For a few years I was completely depressed, physically and mentally. The doctors advised me to go back to Poland, so I started to think how to escape, how to leave Israel.'

She gazed out the window and I had the feeling she wasn't so much talking to me as to herself.

'And so, I arrived back in Warsaw, the city where I spent those happy years with my family. I found my old friends from before the war, met a wonderful, kind man and we had two much-loved children.'

I sat very still on the chair and thought about her words and my late father. What would it have meant to him to know that Hannah had lived?

'My husband passed away a few years ago and my son, a merchant banker, lives with his wife and children in New York. My daughter, a professor of literature at Oxford, lives with her family outside London.'

I could hear the soft rustling of the curtains as they shifted in the breeze from the open window.

My mood had shifted. Now I felt a complex mix of happiness for Hannah that her life had been worth living, and sorrow for all that she had lost – that we had lost. I began to weep, but this time the tears were not just for the suffering she had endured.

'So, that is the story of my life, in brief.' She turned her head and looked out the window and we sat in silence for a moment. It was an easy silence, not awkward. Then she said, 'And now, I want to know about your father: how he survived the uprising, how he escaped from the ghetto, when he left Poland, how he settled in Australia, his family and so much more. He was such a dear man – so funny.'

My Lai

Nelson Butler stepped out of the cyclo, reached into his pocket and handed the driver ten dong. He had arrived at the memorial site of My Lai, a place he never imagined he would see again.

He walked past a large stone sculpture and mosaic wall commemorating the dead. More than forty years ago he had been a willing participant in the mass slaughter of children, women and old men, and even though Lieutenant Calley had been court-martialled and convicted of murder for his wanton violence, Butler still felt immense guilt over his own actions.

That day had never left him – it had taken on the shape of the horrible crime he now knew it to be. Butler could still see bodies floating face down in the brown creek, others lying in pools of blood between the rice paddies.

In the years since then, Vietnam had become his world – he had taken it home with him. It was a world he didn't like, a world he didn't want to be part of, but a world he could not escape.

Now the landscape opened up before him – the patchwork of plush greenery, bougainvillea, palms, banana trees, the water lilies in the creek. The tranquillity and eerie silence contrasted starkly with his memories, and the odours in the air were very different from the smells he remembered.

Butler walked up the stone steps to the museum, past a sign in front of a restored house that had been burnt down by US soldiers on that day in March 1968, killing five family members.

Inside was a wooden table set with bowls, and in the corner of a second room woven baskets were stacked haphazardly, one on top of the other. Dust clouded the windows. Photos and paintings hung from the blotched and patched walls.

There was a portrait of William L. Calley, Lieutenant of Charlie Company, first platoon, with the inscription: 'Who took a lot of lives.' Calley had played a leading role in the massacre. Other photos showed US snipers torching houses, people being shot while trying to escape, a pile of contorted bodies.

There was a plaque on the wall listing the names of people killed by Butler and the other GIs. As he read through the list, Butler sucked in his lips; his head felt heavy on his neck. He thought of the children who would have been middle aged now, with children and grandchildren of their own. All gone. But at the time of the massacre the Vietnamese had simply been 'the enemy'.

Butler felt weak, and sat down on the bench next to the wooden table, staring at the portrait of Lieutenant Calley and remembering his fellow soldiers, the men of Charlie Company.

They had arrived at a hamlet in Quang Ngai Province on 15 March 1968, in the late afternoon, only three months after arriving in Vietnam. A grey mist had settled over the rice fields where the villagers were working. Some children were playing hide-and-seek between the mud houses. From the mess tent the soldiers could see the thatched roofs of the huts. Eventually Butler and the other men settled down for the night.

Butler remembered lying in his tent wondering what the next day would bring. They had come to retaliate, to avenge the death of the popular Sergeant George Cox and two other GIs maimed by a booby trap the previous day. Frustrated, angry and traumatised, Butler and the other men were hell-bent on retribution.

He wondered if the intelligence they had received about an imminent surprise attack was reliable. Colonel Henderson had advised them to regard all civilians as Vietcong or sympathetic to the Vietcong.

Next day the weather was warm and sunny, with a ground fog that soon dissipated. There was an unnerving silence punctuated by an occasional voice, then Butler heard the choppers. The men climbed on board, bound for Son My.

Butler was in no mood to enjoy the morning sun, the paddy fields and fresh blossoms. It was all alien, all threatening, the dense undergrowth, the forest, even the long grass could be hiding the enemy.

Laden with ammunition belt, combat equipment, rations, flak jacket and radio, Butler gripped his rifle and sat with Dawson and Simpson at the door of the chopper, his boots hanging over the edge.

Minutes later, at 6.30 am on Saturday 16 March, they reached their destination. The choppers sped low over the mud huts and rice paddies. Children playing in the streets looked up. The choppers put down not far from the village.

'Men, this is what we've been waiting for – search and destroy. Now is our chance to show the chameleon who is running this war!' barked Lieutenant Calley. 'The Vietcong is two-faced. Young or old, he is slippery. By day he is a villager and by night he is the enemy. Don't trust the chameleon! Just shoot the bastard!'

'Search and destroy – fight and kill,' Butler repeated the words to himself, strengthening his resolve, driving out fear.

He jumped from the helicopter. Dawson and Simpson followed.

They moved through the dense undergrowth towards the village. Ahead of them Butler could hear firing, and soon came upon three children lying on the ground – a young boy with blood pouring from a large cavity in his cheek, a girl with part of her head blown away and a younger girl with a bullet through the back of her neck.

Having reached the outskirts of the village, they came upon a clearing surrounded by coconut palms and thick tropical undergrowth. Butler heard voices – Vietnamese voices. He let fly. 'Come out and fight, you sons of bitches!' he bellowed, strafing the clearing. Dawson scattered bullets, spinning back and forth in a half circle.

Simpson screamed, 'Get the bastards!' and fired into the undergrowth. They advanced, step by step.

Two women lay dead: one on her back, her body riddled with holes leaking blood, the other with a crater the size of a coconut in her side, her face in a pool of blood.

Hearing sniper fire, the three soldiers ducked into the long grass, scanning the dirt track, the forest, the rice paddies. Ten metres ahead they could see one of their own, Carter, blood streaming from a wound in his foot.

Butler, Simpson and Dawson followed the track into the village. Ahead they could hear cries and shouts and the rattle of gunfire. Butler suddenly felt a hot charge explode through his veins. Rage and hate took hold of him. He could smell the Vietcong. He thought he could hear laughter, like chattering monkeys, in the thick jungle ahead. 'You bastards, you fucking chameleons, you fucking laugh at me, do you!' he screamed. 'We're going to teach you cunts a lesson.'

The first building on the right had a thatched roof. Dawson pulled a small bottle of kerosene from his backpack and splashed it over the roof. Flicking his cigarette, he lit the dry thatch and the flames flared up the steep pitch of the roof.

Butler set himself up on the opposite side of the track. Embers were flying in all directions, nipping at his neck, hands, wherever his skin was exposed. Flames lit the sky and thick clouds of smoke obscured his vision. Distorted faces shrieked as he worked the rifle. Villagers ran from their burning huts and he dropped them, one on top of the other.

'Fucking fantastic!' Butler shouted. 'We got those mothers.'

The arrival of a tour bus jolted Butler out of his nightmare. He looked at the bougainvillea and wondered how this village could ever know peace again. It was hard to reconcile the horrors of his memory with this serene place.

He stood up and walked into the restored hut, stopping once again at the plaque listing the victims of the massacre. A Buddhist priest was reciting their names, praying for their souls, and a man stood with his wife, apparently explaining to their children what happened at My Lai.

Butler felt his mood shift from reflection to a more complex mix of sorrow, regret, and guilt – mostly guilt. It felt like a murky black cloud in his mind, growing larger, sucking him in. He suddenly felt unsteady on his feet.

Butler breathed deeply, attempting to calm himself. He felt tormented and undeserving – the lot of many Vietnam vets. Easy to talk about the futility of war, and how it made victims of them all – every long-haired hippy had been spouting that when he came home – but the indiscriminate killing of innocent people was evil, and he'd been part of it.

Watching the father talk to his children, Butler was tempted to try to confess to them that he'd been there. He wanted to talk to them about the events that had somehow led to My Lai, to explain, not justify – how could anything justify what they'd done? He wanted to tell them that he'd been trained to take orders, not to question his commanding officers. He wanted to confess that he'd hungered for the approval and praise of those officers.

But what did that explain? He realised that nothing would be gained by such a confession. The victims were long dead, no words would bring them back and he would never be rid of this guilt. It was his burden to carry – his alone.

Back then he hadn't thought about the morality of what they had done, but soon after his return from the war the sleepless nights had begun. He would wake up crying, shaking, his pyjamas drenched in sweat. Haunted each night by images of friends being shot and hounded by guilt about the innocent children, women and old men Charlie Company had murdered, he became jumpy, impatient, irritable. He'd tried to be a happy family man but a black cloud had descended on him.

In the last forty years the ghosts of his past had haunted him with increasing persistence and at times he thought it would be easier to kill himself. Finally, his wife had said to him, 'You need to go back and face this.'

As he stood there in the museum, the thought crossed his mind that perhaps what he needed to do, once and for all, was to be honest, to admit his wrongdoing and not attempt to excuse or justify his actions. Perhaps admitting his culpability to the Vietnamese family would allow his restless soul to find peace. But what if they couldn't speak English? Despite his time in Vietnam, he knew nothing of the language, except a few numbers, some useless terms and obscenities. But as he turned to address the father, the man looked at him coldly and walked away.

Butler moved to the second room. Sitting on the bench at the table was a Vietnamese woman who looked to be in her seventies. Her face was deeply lined, her expression full of pain.

After a moment's hesitation, he sat down next to her.

Finally, she lifted her head to look at him. 'Where you from?'

Butler felt his stomach grip. 'America,' he said.

'You come long way.'

'In more ways than one.'

They sat in silence for a long while.

At last he said, 'I'm so sorry.' He began to weep, great ragged sobs tearing out of him.

She let him cry, then, after a time, she gently laid her hand on his forearm and looked into his eyes.

Butler felt his shoulders drop and he exhaled, deeply. It was something.

The Other Woman

Isaac and Christina sat chatting on the back verandah. The spring sun warmed the red brick of her old Edwardian home.

'It's a routine procedure,' Isaac said. 'It's only a stent. Doctor Fisher can do it with his eyes closed.' He took another big bite of his bagel.

'I don't care,' Christina insisted. 'I hate hospitals. What if something goes wrong? It's your heart, for god's sake.'

'I'll be fine,' Isaac said, a little impatiently. 'Nothing's going to change. I'll still be here every Sunday, banging on about asylum seekers and refugees.'

'How long will you be in hospital? Can I come and visit you?'

'I don't think that would be a good idea,' Isaac said gently. 'Paula and the kids might be there.'

Christina stood up, went to the kitchen and returned to the verandah with a pot of tea. 'Promise you'll ring me on Tuesday morning to let me know everything went okay.'

'Of course.'

Just then, David ran onto the veranda. 'Dad, can we go to the park for a kick?'

'Sure. How about we go now while the sun is out?'

David tucked the football under his arm and reached for his

father's hand, dancing along and tugging at Isaac to hurry. 'What's the matter, Dad? Why are you puffing?'

Age had taken its toll on Isaac's athleticism, and his once-slender torso had thickened. His grey hair looked distinguished, but he was a heavy man, thick in the body and red-faced.

'I've been short of breath lately and the doctor has booked me in for a procedure tomorrow to fix it.'

'Can I still see you next week?' David asked.

'Of course. I'm not sure I'll be able to play footy but I'll come over for brunch as usual,' Isaac said as he ruffled David's hair affectionately.

On Tuesday morning Christina woke early. She had had a restless night, so instead of opening the curtains as she usually did to let in the day, she lay in darkness, pulling the covers up to her ears and dozing. When she next woke, the red eyes of the clock said 7.30 am. She had to take David to school and there was shopping to do, but Isaac's procedure stood like a monolith in her mind.

She got up, dressed, and went to the kitchen to make David's breakfast.

'Your jumper's inside out,' David said as he walked through the kitchen door.

'Oh, silly me.'

'Are you okay?'

'I didn't sleep very well last night,' she sighed. 'I was thinking about Dad and the operation. I'm worried about him.'

When Christina arrived at Ormond Primary School, David opened the car door, looked at his mother and said, 'Don't worry Mum, Dad'll be okay.'

Tuesdays were Christina's day off. She worked at the local library, and often did voluntary work at the church in her spare time, but today she felt heavy-hearted and lethargic – she just couldn't face it. Instead, she drove to Smith Street, her favourite shopping strip in Melbourne, hoping for distraction. She meandered aimlessly along the street, looking at artisan jewellery and second-hand books, but nothing satisfied her; she couldn't get her mind off Isaac. Giving up, she went to Woolworths for the weekly groceries, passing drug addicts and busking hipsters. She wandered back towards the car, a knot of anxiety in her stomach that she couldn't ease.

It was 11.30 when she got back to the house. She turned on the radio and sat in the lounge in Isaac's favourite chair. Then she got up and stood in front of the gas heater in the dining room. She felt chilled to the bone even though there were blossoms on the trees and the early spring day was fine.

She reached into her handbag to check her phone again. It wasn't there. Isaac had rung and she'd missed his call! She ran to the car, where she was sure she'd left it, allowing herself to feel momentarily relieved. But when she looked at the screen, there were no missed calls or messages. Her heart pounded.

By now it was twelve o'clock. Isaac was usually so reliable she was convinced something was wrong.

To distract herself Christina went to David's bedroom. Lifting a disorderly pile of T-shirts and singlets, she began stacking them on a shelf in the cupboard. Then she hung up David's jeans and pants, making sure the coathangers were evenly spaced and facing in the same direction. It calmed her to concentrate on this small task.

She left the bedroom, walked back to the lounge, stood at the window and gazed at her camellias. Then she took out the vacuum cleaner and ran it over the carpet, even though she'd vacuumed the previous day.

Suddenly, in a decisive movement, she picked up the phone and rang the hospital.

'Can I speak to Isaac Friedman please?'

'Who's calling?' the nurse asked.

'My name is Christina.'

'What is your relationship to Mr Friedman?'

She paused. 'I'm his sister,' she said.

There was a moment of silence and then the nurse said, 'I'm very sorry, Christina, hasn't anyone told you?'

'Told me what?'

'I'm sorry to have to tell you, but Mr Friedman suffered a heart attack during the procedure and passed away early this morning.'

Christina felt her face grow hot and the blood beat in her head. Her chest felt tight. She slumped into a chair and tried to make sense of what the nurse had just told her.

When she next looked at her watch it was two o'clock. She picked up the phone and called Sarah, her best friend.

'Sarah, Isaac is dead.'

'What do you mean? What happened?'

'He went to the hospital for a procedure, and he had a heart attack and died.'

'I'm so sorry,' Sarah said quietly.

'What do I do?' Christina cried. 'I won't even know when the funeral is … or where!'

'Do you intend to go?' Sarah asked tentatively.

'I'd like to … but what do you think?'

Sarah paused and said, 'Given the circumstances it's a bit tricky. To Isaac you were everything, but to the outside world you don't exist. Sorry to be so blunt.'

'I know, and you're right … But I loved him! I can't miss his funeral. And what about David?'

'Do what you need to do Christina. I understand,' Sarah said.

'What if I stand at the back? No one will even know I'm there.'

'Would you like me to come?' Sarah said.

'Thank you for offering, Sarah, but I'll take David – I think it should be just the two of us.'

'Take care of yourself,' Sarah said gently.

At 3.30, David returned from school. Christina hadn't felt capable of leaving the house so she had asked her neighbour to pick him up.

When David opened the car door Christina was staring out the window into the street, resting her forehead against the glass.

'What's the matter, Mum?' he asked, as he came into the lounge.

Christina turned and looked at him. A sob lurched from her. She couldn't get the words out. Swallowing hard, she took a breath.

'Your father passed away this morning,' she said, looking at David with wet eyes. Her words seemed to echo through the house.

'What do you mean? What happened?'

'Remember Dad told you he was having a procedure? Well, he had a heart attack during the surgery.'

David put his arms around his mother and sobbed.

After a long time, Christina pulled back and said, 'I've decided to go to the funeral, David. I would very much like you to be there with me, if you feel up to it.'

'Of course I do, Mum.'

Arriving at the cemetery dressed in customary black, her face concealed by a veil beneath a black hat, Christina was surprised to see that she and David were the only mourners dressed in such a way. Hundreds of people, mostly in casual clothes, had gathered at the steps of the chapel.

Who are all these people? Christina wondered. What did they share with him? Although she had always known it, now it hit her with a new force that Isaac had had a whole other life, a community of family and friends that she knew nothing about. In that moment she felt very estranged from him.

Grabbing David's hand, she said, 'Maybe we should go … I'm not sure I can do this.'

'We're here now, Mum,' David said quietly. 'We should pay our last respects to Dad.'

Taking a deep breath to strengthen her resolve, Christina nodded and she and David followed the congregation into the chapel, taking a seat in the back row. David noticed that all the men were sitting separately from the women, so he got up and walked to the other side of the chapel. When he sat down a man approached and offered him a skullcap. David dutifully placed it on his head.

At the front of the chapel the coffin, draped with a black cloth embroidered with the Star of David, rested on a trolley in front of the podium. A woman, who Christina assumed was Isaac's wife, and two teenage children walked in and sat beside the coffin.

When the rabbi entered, the murmur in the room died down and the chapel fell silent. The rabbi read from his memorial prayer book, initially in Hebrew, then in English. 'How blessed are those who reject the advice of the wicked, don't stand on the way of sinners or sit where scoffers sit … O Lord, who may abide in your tent … he who walks with integrity, and works righteousness and speaks truth in his heart … nor does evil to his neighbour …'

Hearing these sacred words, Christina hoped that, despite Isaac's double life, God would look kindly on him. She knew that Isaac was a good man with a kind heart.

Isaac's brother, Henry, delivered the eulogy, his voice husky. Resting his elbows on the lectern, he leaned forward and spoke about Isaac's determination to preserve his Jewish heritage, his loyalty as a brother and his generosity towards his family. Adjusting his glasses, he concluded by saying, 'My brother came with our family to this country as a young boy to escape anti-Semitism, he studied and became a well-respected human-rights lawyer.' Then, with glazed eyes, he stopped, walked to the coffin and rested his hands on it. 'I will never forget you,' he sobbed.

In the chapel there was absolute silence. All eyes were fixed on Henry as he returned to the podium. 'My brother was a mensch.'

Christina studied the faces of the congregation, each one etched in grief and shock at Isaac's untimely and unexpected passing. She was glad to be amongst these people who felt just as she did. It was a comfort.

When the rabbi asked for pallbearers, Henry and five other men walked towards the coffin and hoisted it on to their shoulders. Then they led the funeral march to the gravesite. The congregation filed out of the chapel and followed behind. After waiting a few moments, Christina and David joined them, walking slowly at the back of the procession.

When the mourners arrived at the grave, the pallbearers rested the coffin on two planks of wood that straddled the grave. Ropes were placed under the coffin, the planks removed and the coffin lowered into the ground. The rabbi said the memorial prayer.

Christina stared at the coffin lying in the earth. It was a confronting sight. Again, she squeezed David's hand to comfort them both.

At the rabbi's word, Isaac's wife raised the spade and the first clod of dirt hit the coffin. Hearing the hollow sound of gravel falling on wood, Christina felt her chest tighten and blood rush to her temples. Every other funeral she'd attended had been a cremation; this Jewish burial was foreign to her – a brutal, shocking tradition that made no attempt to shield mourners from the finality of death. She became acutely aware of the biblical phrase, 'From dust to dust'.

Suddenly, Isaac's Jewishness – which she had been only remotely aware of during their relationship – overwhelmed her. Not only was he part of a community that she knew nothing about, but now his religion put up another barrier and separated him from her even further. She turned to David, who seemed fascinated by the ritual of each mourner taking a turn to shovel soil onto the coffin.

'I want to do it too, Mum,' he whispered.

Shaking her head, Christina said, 'Please stay with me, David, I need you here.'

Once the burial was over, the mourners filed along the pathway to the exit, offering their condolences to Isaac's family as they passed. His wife clutched a handkerchief, dabbing at her eyes as she wept. His son, however, was stony-faced, obviously numb with shock at his father's sudden death.

Needing a private moment with Isaac, Christina walked back to the grave with David. She wanted to recapture something of their intimacy, something independent of all these people and their foreign rituals.

After a few moments, she felt someone touch her forearm. Turning, she came face to face with Isaac's wife.

'I'm sorry, we haven't met,' Paula said. The woman's face was ashen, a darkness around her eyes.

'I'm Paula, Isaac's wife.' Paula was looking at her curiously, but Christina couldn't meet her gaze.

'I'm wondering how you knew my husband?' Paula said, her eyes fixed on David.

Christina felt the cold, sharp air on her cheeks and shivered. 'Oh, ah, I knew him from—'

'He's my dad,' David said bluntly, and the tears began to roll down his cheeks once more.

'What?' Paula said, her voice trembling. 'Your dad? But …'

Christina felt the blood rush to her face. She grabbed David's hand. 'I'm sorry,' she mumbled, 'we have to go.'

It had happened, she thought as she and David walked quickly to the car, the worst, the very worst. Her cover was blown. In her state of blind panic she couldn't contemplate where this might lead or what harm had been done.

Henry drove Paula and the children out through the cemetery gates onto Dandenong Road and turned towards home, where she had invited the mourners for refreshments.

She'd lived here with Isaac for the past twenty years. Paula glanced around at a house that suddenly seemed unfamiliar and made straight for the couch where she sat down with a heavy sigh. Henry, his wife Judy and her friends and family were talking, their conversation hushed. Paula wasn't listening. She drank coffee and fiddled with food she couldn't eat, until she'd had enough. She excused herself and said to Henry, 'I'm tired, it's been a long day. Do you mind keeping your eye on the children if I lie down for half an hour? Wake me if I'm needed.'

That night she lay in their familiar bed in the familiar bedroom but it felt utterly strange. The room seemed big and cold without Isaac's warmth. She turned her face to the wall and sobbed. Eventually, Paula fell asleep, but at three in the morning she woke, and the face she saw was Christina's.

Could it be true? Was Isaac really that boy's father? Perhaps that was why she'd noticed him. Was Isaac capable of having an affair? He was an honest man, moral, with a strong set of ethics – or so she'd thought.

Paula got up and shuffled to the kitchen to get a glass of water. She felt like an old woman. Sitting down at the kitchen table, forcing herself to be honest, she reflected on her relationship with her husband.

The truth was, she and Isaac were no longer close. Their sexual intimacy had faded years ago. She knew it had bothered him; he had tried to talk to her many times, but she had shut down the conversation. She hated talking about sex – it made her uncomfortable – and since menopause she had lost all interest. Occasionally she acquiesced, but it was a chore. Over the last twelve years they had settled into a polite and quiet life: they took care of each other when one of them was sick; they bought each other flowers and gifts on their wedding anniversaries,
birthdays and other occasions. There was respect and kindness between them, but no passion.

Paula thought about their weekends – Isaac's determination to keep Sundays to himself. She remembered his impatience when she questioned him, his refusal to compromise, his insistence that he needed his 'down time'.

If she was really honest with herself, could she blame Isaac for seeking sexual intimacy elsewhere? Perhaps it was due to Christina that Isaac had accepted the lack of sex in their marriage? Because of her, he had not demanded it from Paula. Maybe, Paula thought, in a strange kind of paradox, Christina had saved her marriage with Isaac.

Hour after hour, she sat in the dark kitchen, contemplating what she had discovered. She couldn't get over the fact that Isaac had had an affair, that he had a son whom she knew nothing about. Somehow that seemed a more painful betrayal.

She wondered how Isaac knew this woman. Had he met her at gym, or golf? Or was she a mother at school? No, that boy was younger than their children.

The more she thought about it, the stronger was her intuition that the woman must be a client.

Paula got into her car at 7 am and drove to Isaac's legal practice in the city. Alone in the office, she searched her mind for Isaac's password. After trying the children's names, she typed in Carlton – his football club of many years. Success. She accessed his records, and after an hour or so she discovered – shockingly, but also unsurprisingly – a trail of emails between her husband and Christina. Not only did they disclose her voluntary work with asylum seekers but also conversations of a very personal nature. Paula felt a shiver run through her and found herself clutching a pen as if it were a weapon. The ridges of her knuckles had turned white and her jaw was clenched with anger.

Getting up from her chair, Paula paced through the empty rooms of the practice, her head spinning. After a few moments, she paused to gather her thoughts and then walked decisively to the reception area and turned on the computer. Going back through Isaac's database, she eventually found Christina's address.

Her heart was pounding as she pulled up in front of the house. Gathering her resolve, she walked up the path that led to the front door and rang the bell.

Christina's thin face paled when she opened the door. After a moment she said, 'Hello Paula. Please come in.'

Paula followed Christina down the hall to the lounge, trying to hold her nerve as she noticed a photo of Isaac, Christina and the boy hanging on the wall. It was all so surreal. Here she was in a strange house with a woman she had just met, and there was a photo of her husband and his son on the wall. She wanted to put her fist through the glass.

'Take a seat. Can I offer you coffee?' Christina asked, her voice shaking.

Ignoring her question, Paula looked at Christina for a long moment. 'How could you?' she said through gritted teeth.

Taken aback at Paula's bluntness, Christina finally said, 'I'm sorry for the pain this has caused you.'

At that moment David walked into the room. He was similar in build to her own son, with sand-coloured hair, a lean face and a square jaw. She looked into his eyes and saw a kind and gentle soul.

Paula was disarmed. She took a deep breath. A shiver ran through her.

'This is my son, David,' Christina said, motioning the boy to sit down next to her. He did so quietly, his hands in his lap.

No one spoke, the silence seeming to fill the room with a noise of its own. But Christina couldn't let the silence continue. Searching for something to say, she offered, 'We're such complicated things – people, I mean, are complicated …' Her words trailed off, aimless, disconnected.

Paula looked into herself, searching for strength. She stared at Christina, not knowing what to think or how to respond. She felt numb.

Christina turned to David and said, 'Go into the kitchen and have a glass of milk. You can have chocolate syrup if you like.'

When David left the room Christina took a deep breath and began to talk slowly about Isaac, choosing her words carefully.

Paula listened in silence and heard the pain in her voice as she spoke about their life together, their intimate, human dealings, and their beloved son. Christina told her everything.

Paula watched her tremble, saw her eyes brimming with tears and knew what she was trying to say. Her own anger had melted away when she heard of their love for Isaac and the agony of their loss. She managed to remain silent. As Christina spoke Paula felt more and more sympathetic – she knew exactly what they were feeling about Isaac.

Then Christina smiled faintly, apologetically. She looked at Paula, started to speak, then stopped. She buried her face in her hands and sobbed. The sound tore apart the silence in the room and shook her body. Paula went over to her and put her arm around her shoulders and felt her trembling. And then Paula was crying too, for the pain of their loss, their suffering and their love for Isaac.

Refugees

'Have you heard the news this morning?' Paul said as I pulled back my chair and sat down at our regular café for breakfast. 'The minister's been banging on about refugees again.'

Paul and I were close friends. As kids we had gone to school together, shared tennis and music lessons, and each summer attended the same school holiday programs. Now, as surgeons in our senior years, we had been meeting at this same café for breakfast each Saturday for as long as I could remember. We talked regularly about everything from the state of the economy to our prized grandchildren.

'No, what's he been saying?' I asked, looking across the table at my old friend.

'The usual nonsense about refugees who come to our country and threaten our security.'

'Hang on a sec,' I said, sitting upright in my chair and frowning in disagreement. 'What's wrong with us deciding who comes to this country? Look at what's been happening in Europe!'

As soon as I spoke I realised I should have kept quiet. Paul and I usually avoided talking politics. As far back as our university days we'd had different opinions on many social and political issues. Apart from our common interest in medicine and girls, he was absorbed in literature and politics and I was interested in sport. While I was training for the triathlon, Paul was handing out leaflets and explaining with passionate conviction why the upcoming referendum giving Aboriginal people the right to be counted in the census was so important. 'It will allow the federal government to make laws for Aboriginal people and prevent the state and federal governments cheating them out of their rights,' he explained to me one evening at dinner.

At university we often sat in the cafeteria drinking coffee, Paul listening to every word I, and others, said, careful not to interrupt, waiting patiently to speak, never raising his voice and never pretending to know better.

'We've stopped taking children from their parents because they're black,' Paul said, on one occasion. 'Now we take them because they're living in squalor. But we spend more money on surveillance and removing kids than we spend supporting their families.'

Irrespective of whether or not I agreed with Paul, I always admired his courage in standing up for what he believed to be right, his determination to make changes for the better and his good intentions. He was considered, considerate and inspiring, and while I often disagreed with him, I respected him.

'Anyway, it's not nonsense; our security is important,' I added.

'Of course it's important, but refugees don't threaten it,' Paul countered.

I shook my head, opened my mouth and then closed it. Paul looked at me and for a moment neither of us spoke.

Breaking the silence, I said, 'How can you say that?'

Paul hesitated. 'According to the Refugee Council of Australia, since 2009, ASIO has listed adverse security assessments to less than one per cent of boat arrivals.'

I stared at him, lost for words. Paul was well read, grounded and reliable, and I knew what he said would be correct. I felt embarrassed.

'This means, of course,' he persisted, 'ninety-nine per cent of refugees have passed the security checks required for the granting of a protection visa.'

After breakfast I took pleasure in the brisk autumn air and walked the few blocks to my car. Driving home along St Kilda Road, bored and frustrated by the gridlocked traffic, I thought about my breakfast conversation with Paul and started to grapple with why I had formed such a strong anti-refugee viewpoint.

Maybe it was because most of the refugees who come to Australia were from Afghanistan and other Muslim countries and I tended to assume they'd bring with them virulent anti-Semitic sentiments. This no doubt had its roots in my childhood and the experience of my parents and grandparents, who were the victims of anti-Semitism during the Second World War.

The embers of my childhood flared into life once more. I recalled my first experience with anti-Semitism. One lunchtime at primary school I was eating my pastrami and pickle on rye bread when John, the school bully, and a few of his mates came sauntering towards me. They surrounded me, and John stepped up and knocked the sandwich out of my hand. 'Bloody Jew,' he snarled. 'Piss off.'

Behind them I saw Mrs Collins across the quadrangle walking towards us. I motioned with my head. 'Look behind you,' I said, fuming, but trying to appear calm. He turned to see Mrs Collins bearing down on him, stole a quick glance at me and then jerked his head at the others. As he walked off he raised his middle finger and said, 'You'll keep.'

Every day there seemed to be some little jab – a look, a raised finger – to remind me of their contempt. I've never forgotten it.

I realised that those childhood experiences – the way people avoided our family in the street, or watched us picnicking at the park, smiling politely but never speaking to us – informed the way I saw migrants. It made no sense, but there you are. I stared at the road, shifted uneasily in my seat, and wondered whether my prejudices were justified or simply irrational fears.

When I arrived home, my wife Judy was standing at the living-room window, waiting for me. As I opened the door and walked inside she looked at me and smiled. 'How was your morning, Stephen?'

'Very thought-provoking,' I said. 'At breakfast, Paul and I got into an argument about refugees. But then, driving home, I started to think about why I have such disdain for refugees.'

'And?'

'And I thought about being bullied at school.'

Judy nodded, indicating I should continue.

'I think when my family escaped Europe and arrived in Australia they were desperate to put the past behind them. They wanted to fit in, and in the process they distanced themselves from being refugees. So much so that I realise they have a profound lack of empathy. That's how I was brought up.'

I saw Judy watching me closely, her eyes gentle.

'I guess it's a bit like children who are beaten growing up to become brutal parents, or children who are sexually abused growing up to be paedophiles.'

'Hmm . . . I've never heard you speak sympathetically about refugees,' she said quietly. There was a long silence, then Judy leaned forward and looked me in the eye. 'What's interesting is that you and Paul share a holocaust background, but while you feel victimised and fearful, Paul doesn't. I wonder why he's not afraid of a flood of anti-Semites in the way you are.'

I looked at Judy and considered her words, but before I could answer she went on, 'He's much more compassionate and sympathetic to the plight of refugees than you are.'

'Thanks.' I felt my jaw clench.

'Remember that discussion at the Jewish Museum when Paul talked about the members of his family who'd been on the St Louis in 1939 when it was forced to return to Europe? And we all know what happened to the passengers on that ship. Most were slaughtered because they were Jewish.'

'Yes,' I said in a small voice. 'I also had family on that ship.'

'That heartless act has obviously informed his views,' Judy said.

I thought for a moment and said, 'Paul has always been left-wing. If you remember, he marched against the Vietnam War and supported Jack Mundey's campaign to preserve historic houses long before it was fashionable. But he's naive about what goes on in the real world – still a bit of a hippy really.'

The following day I got an early-morning briefing from the surgical registrar of the Emergency Department before I left for the hospital. I immediately went to examine my first patient, an Iraqi doctor who'd been the victim of a ferocious knife attack. 'Apparently three masked men broke into his house and knifed him, again and again. The paramedics said there were anti-refugee slogans sprayed all over the walls.'

'What?'

'It's just lucky his family were away at the time.'

I put on my scrubs, washed my hands and as I walked towards the theatre I concentrated on the briefing – stabilised by the resuscitation team . . . pulse . . . blood pressure . . . breathing . . . drip and fluids for shock . . . anaesthetist at the ready.

In the centre of the room, a man was lying on the operating table, blood-soaked bandages wrapped around his torso. He looked familiar, in his mid-fifties, dark hair and eyes, heavy black stubble.

'Let's have a look – ultrasound?' I said to the theatre sister as she removed the bandages.

My assistant Meg tensed as the extent of the wounds to the patient's torso was revealed. 'I know this man,' she said. 'He's an orthopaedic surgeon, a world authority. I've worked with him.'

Suddenly, I was looking at myself lying flat on my back with my chest and belly ruptured – a surgeon, just like this man. I was every one of my family who'd been brutalised and hurt by the Nazis. It shook me to my core.

'Let's locate all the wounds,' I said sternly, struggling to regain some control and calm. 'We don't want to miss any.'

'Let's locate all the wounds. We don't want to miss any.'

As we worked, the sister said quietly, 'He came to Australia about twenty years ago I think. His work on prosthetics has put Australia on the map.'

The operation took five hours. I left Meg to finish off the sutures and dress the wounds, briefed her on his post-operative care, which she knew as well as I did, then left the theatre.

I peeled off my scrubs and rinsed my hands, feeling a film of perspiration on my forehead and upper lip. I splashed water over my face and neck and walked to the window as I dried off. I wondered if things might have been different for my patient if the government did not call refugees 'illegal' and force them to live for years in squalid detention centres. How would I have coped in such circumstances? The government was sending a message to every racist and white supremacist that refugees were second-class citizens. It gave bigots a licence to treat refugees with contempt.

I put on my glasses, then took them off and wiped my eyes. I felt uneasy. I realised I was not proud of my government's refugee policy.

It was late so I called Judy and picked up some takeaway from our favourite local Vietnamese restaurant on the way home. As I opened the door Judy wrapped her arms around me and gave me a hard hug that left me breathless. 'Yum,' she said, 'you smell delicious.'

'That's the dinner, not me,' I said with a smile.

'What kept you?' Judy said. 'I've been home for hours.'

'I'm exhausted, it's been a tough day,' I said, dumping the bags on the bench.

'You can tell me all about it over dinner – let's help ourselves. I've set the table.'

I followed Judy to the table and started unpacking the takeaway cartons.

'Wine?' Judy asked.

'Please.'

While we ate, I was aware of Judy looking at me, waiting for me to tell her about my day. After a few mouthfuls of wine, and with the food starting to fill my empty insides, I felt able to share with her the details of what had happened to the patient I had operated on.

'I performed a five-hour operation on a well-known refugee who was the victim of a racist attack,' I told her.

She looked shocked, then after a moment she said quietly, 'Will he be okay? Who is he?'

'Yes, I'm sure we saved his life,' I said.

She smiled at me and said, 'You should feel very pleased with yourself.'

'But it's made me think about how we treat refugees in this country and how irresponsible the government is in promoting its refugee policy – it's so harsh . . .'

She looked at me for a moment then said, 'I agree with you.'

The following Saturday was sunny and warm. I arrived at Darling Street Café and found Paul at our usual table drinking an orange juice.

Lifting his head from the newspaper, he fixed me with a questioning eye and said, 'Why the cheeky grin?'

'I have a confession to make,' I said.

'What's that?' he said, raising an eyebrow.

'Before I go on, let me tell you about my week.'

He folded up his newspaper and nodded, indicating I should continue.

'On Monday morning I operated on a refugee, a really impressive guy.'

Paul looked at me expectantly.

I hesitated for a moment and said, 'He was the victim of a vicious attack by white supremacists. They almost killed him.'

'So do I detect the start of a change of attitude?' Paul prodded.

I swallowed hard and said in a small voice, 'It's made me think carefully about my views.'

A faint smile began to play around the corners of his mouth.

I leaned forward and said, 'The events of this week have forced me to examine some of my attitudes; I feel my views have softened.' I paused before continuing, waiting for Paul's response, but he just nodded expectantly. 'And I've also come to understand that each time the government ramps up its hysterical anti-refugee rhetoric, it tacitly gives licence to racists to express their hatred.'

Paul stared at me for a long moment, seeming to absorb the import of my words. Then he said, 'Sometimes life moves in mysterious ways. It teaches us what we need to learn at exactly the right time.'

Shabbat

Friday – the night Jewish people commemorate the Sabbath. On this Shabbat, as on countless other Friday nights, John registered the strange unease he always felt in his mother's house. He had grown up here, and yet it never felt like home. The feeling had grown even stronger after his father's death, when it slowly dawned on John how much his father's warmth and generosity of spirit had enlivened the family.

Sitting at the heavy mahogany table in the dining room, he gazed through the doorway into his mother's study: the shelves of books in alphabetical order, the thick Persian rug, the wheeled stepladder with trinkets or ornaments on each step.

Sarah, his mother, entered the room and bent to kiss him. 'Good Shabbos,' she said.

John inclined his head stiffly. 'Good Shabbos,' he replied, then abruptly stood up. 'Just getting a glass of water,' he said, unable to meet her eye.

Returning from the kitchen, John studied Sarah covertly as she finished setting the table, placing napkins in engraved rings and gleaming silver coasters on the embroidered white linen tablecloth. These last few months he'd noticed a heaviness, almost a lethargy in her movements, but that was hardly surprising: she was eighty-seven.

For years her hearing had been so bad she had strained to make out conversations, and now, with her large eyes sunk into dark sockets, she looked quite ill.

John heard the front door open.

'Good Shabbos,' his brother called, his voice echoing down the hall, as he ushered his wife and their two sons, Benjamin and Mark, into the room.

They exchanged the customary greetings, then John turned to Benjamin. 'Mazel-tov,' he said, 'I hear you passed your exams.'

Benjamin grinned, but before he could say anything, John's two children, Rebecca and Joshua, arrived with his wife Deborah. 'Sorry we're late,' she said, 'we waited until the rain eased.'

That Shabbat, like every other, candles stood in silver candlesticks at the head of the table beside the challah and wine. The family was observant, steeped in tradition, treasuring its history, and the customary Jewish way of life. They believed in God, ate kosher food and observed the Sabbath, festivals and holy days. At John's insistence, and despite her protests about being the centre of attention, Sarah agreed to sit at the head of the Shabbat table. For her part, it was an honour she would never have chosen, preferring to remain quietly unnoticed.

John, the younger of Sarah's two sons, sat on her right next to his wife. Maurice, the elder, sat on her left beside his wife, and the four grandchildren, all now young teenagers, were grouped together at the end of the table.

John's daughter Rebecca lit the candles, welcomed the Sabbath and sang the blessing. John lifted the wine glass and said, 'Barukh atah Adonai, Eloheinu, melekh ha-olam, borei p'ri hagafen.' And translated for the children, 'Praise to You, our God, Sovereign of the universe, Creator of the fruit of the vine.'

John's nephew Mark removed the cover from the challah while reciting the blessing over the bread.

Sarah smiled, glanced at her granddaughter and asked, 'How was school?' Then, before Rebecca could reply, turned to Deborah and said, 'And how was your day?' Not for the first time John considered this woman who talked but said nothing of real significance and seemed unable to listen. Was it just her deafness?

John watched as his mother rested her chin on her palm to hide the faint tremor. She must have been a beauty in her youth, and even in old age she was still striking.

Deborah smiled and said, 'Fine, thanks, and Rebecca handed in that history project, didn't you, honey.'

'I'm doing a history project, too,' Josh offered, 'on my roots. Can I interview you about the war, Nana?'

'No,' Sarah said decisively, and reached for the chopped liver, concentrating a little too hard as she spread it on her challah.

John thought of the many times he had asked his mother the same question, and how she had invariably shut down the conversation or abruptly changed the subject.

Joshua glanced at his mother, puzzled by his grandmother's blunt response.

'Great herring salad, Nana,' Rebecca said, to ease the tension.

'All the other kids in the class are getting help from their grandparents,' Joshua persisted, staring at his grandmother.

'Isn't it time you talked about it, Sarah?' Deborah said gently.

'Yes, Nana, what happened?' said Benjamin.

Sarah muttered to herself, took another bite of challah, then said, 'Enough. I don't want to talk about it.' Her eyes had gone dead, and John realised he had seen this expression on his mother's face before. Her whole face became impassive, blank. She got to her feet wearily. 'Some things should not be talked about,' she said, then left the table and disappeared into the kitchen.

John had no idea of his family history; his whole life had been lived in the shadow of his mother's secrets. His father had talked openly about his own family, mourning the losses, celebrating the few survivals. But his mother had remained mute. Didn't Joshua have a right to know about his heritage? Didn't John himself?

That night John couldn't sleep. He lay beside Deborah and thought about his family's Shabbat meal, his jaw and neck tight as he retraced the conversation.

What was his mother hiding? He thought about her obsession with cleanliness, her insistence that the dusting be done daily, the effort she put into polishing all the silverware till it gleamed.

John recalled a rare beach holiday they'd had when he was a little boy. His mother had scraped a line in the wet sand to mark the boundary of his playground. Of course he'd crossed the line, running gleefully into the towering waves, her hoarse shrieks muffled by the roar of the surf. She'd dragged him roughly from the water, slapped him hard on the backside, her eyes full of panic, her chest heaving from exertion. He'd been frightened of her, but now he realised that her overreaction was an expression of her own dark inner terrors. Remembering her response to Joshua, he realised how rigidly she guarded those terrors.

He eased himself out of bed to fetch a glass of water, resolving to speak to his mother. Joshua had a right to know the family history – they all did. After so many years, he could no longer tolerate his mother's silence. He suddenly felt an urgent need to know her, to try one last time to establish the intimacy that had eluded him throughout his life. After all, they had very little time left.

Next morning John went to see his mother. She opened the door in her loose-fitting pink nightgown, her face stripped of makeup. She looked weary, vulnerable and small. Although she was surprised to see him, she didn't comment on his unannounced visit.

'Can I come in?' John asked after a short silence.

'Of course.' She stepped back and ushered him into the house.

Taking a seat at the kitchen table, John said, 'We need to talk.'

'If it is about last night, there is nothing to say,' Sarah said. 'You want coffee?'

'Thank you. And yes, there is. You upset Joshua.'

'I know, I know,' Sarah sighed. 'I'm sorry. I don't know …'

Looking at his frail old mother, John was momentarily lost for words. How to begin to ask the questions that had for so long gone unasked?

'Tell me about your parents,' he said suddenly, before he had time to think.

Sarah's eyes narrowed. 'Why? What purpose does it serve?' She was quiet a long time, staring blankly out of the window.

John watched her, patiently waiting for her to speak.

Eventually she sighed heavily. 'All right,' she said brusquely. 'My father was a merchant – a successful businessman, self-made. He imported silk from Italy and France into Poland. He was a cultured man. He had seats at the theatre and the opera and he would host politicians and visitors from abroad. Yitzhak Gruenbaum, the leader of the Zionist faction in the Polish Parliament, loved going to the opera, and often accompanied my parents. Our family had influence. We had respectability … status. In Warsaw, before Hitler, we were the social elite.'

John leaned in as Sarah spoke, encouraged, even astonished, that she had finally shared some small part of her past.

'Did you live in a big house?' he asked.

Sarah regarded John silently for several moments. 'What do you want from me?' she said.

John held her gaze, waiting for her to continue.

'We had an apartment, on the third floor,' she said, leaning her forearms on the table. 'It overlooked a boulevard lined with big trees. It was not like the Jewish area – the plantation in the centre had shrubs and flowers. When I sat at the piano in the living room I could look out over the park. The rooms were big, with high ceilings, and we had paintings – some beautiful paintings. My mother had a maidservant to polish her silver and clean the crystal. My father sent us to a Jewish school and employed private tutors to come to our home to teach us drawing or music. He employed a French governess to teach us French and needlework and take us to school. My sister was two years older than me. Each Friday a man would do errands for our family.' She paused thoughtfully. 'We had a good life … and we were happy. My parents were kind …' Her voice faded and she stared unseeing at her hands, twisting and crumpling some invisible cloth.

John hesitated, then took a deep breath and said, 'Tell me what happened.'

Sarah reached for her coffee cup, her hand trembling. When she finally spoke, her voice was husky and low.

'One day my father asked me to run an errand. I was fifteen.' She took a sip of coffee.

'The Nazis snatched me off the street,' she said. 'I was taken to Nazi headquarters. They had the lot there – crystal chandeliers, wood-panelling, paintings, mirrors … I remember there were waiters carrying trays of wine and beer, and the men were singing.' Sarah seemed lost in thought. I remember the uniforms, the red armbands, the black leather boots … swastikas …'

John leant across and took her hand, stroking the thin papery skin. It was the first time he had touched her hand in years.

'They escorted me from the room … they took turns,' she said, tears running down the lines in her cheeks.

John tried to imagine the terror of a fifteen-year-old girl, momentarily pictured his own daughter, but shied away from the image in revulsion.

'I lost count of the number of nights,' Sarah said, her voice cracking.

John felt a dark horror move through him.

'One morning I went to the bathroom, grabbed a razor blade, and cut off great chunks of my hair until I was almost bald. That afternoon three of them raped me. That was my punishment,' she continued.

John looked at his mother, his eyes filled with tears. 'I'm so sorry,' he said hoarsely. It was all he could think of to say.

'After the war I learned about the gas chambers of Treblinka, Auschwitz, and the mass slaughter of Jews in the Ponary Forest,' Sarah continued.

John tried to think about the murdered millions, but it was too vast, too appalling. His own mother's suffering was less easy to evade.

The Nazis might have tried to destroy Sarah's spirit, but her children and grandchildren were testament to her defiance of the Nazis' genocidal aspirations. Some words from My Name is

Asher Lev came to him then: 'To kill a human being is to kill also the children and children's children that might have come from him down through all the generations.'

'I never spoke about what happened to me,' Sarah explained. 'I couldn't. It was the only way I could live. More than anything, I think about my parents and what they must have felt that night when I didn't return. I never saw them again. They all died without knowing I had survived.'

John was overwhelmed with compassion for his mother. Finally he asked her, 'And Dad, did he know?'

Sarah placed her trembling hands in her lap. 'I told him. I had to,' she said. 'It … affected us.'

John swallowed hard, his head starting to pound, and a heaviness gathered in his chest. 'I'll just be a moment,' he said, walking down the hallway to the bathroom. He splashed water on his face, collected himself and returned to the kitchen.

'You try to convince yourself that you are a victim, that it's not your fault,' Sarah continued, 'but deep down you feel guilty – soiled. It weighed on me, ate at me like a cancer.'

'Guilty? What do you mean guilty?' John asked.

'Guilty that I couldn't give your father what he needed,' Sarah said, her head bowed.

John put his arm around his mother and felt her frail shoulders lose a little of their tension. She seemed emotionally depleted, but perhaps this unburdening after so many years would eventually bring her some relief.

'You've carried this for so long – almost your entire life. You needed to talk, Mum,' he said gently.

Lifting her head, Sarah smiled wanly at her son. She reached for the challah from the previous night and tore off a piece. 'I love seeing you all,' she said, before taking a bite, 'my family, my grandchildren, with their smiles, their laughter … I love Shabbat.'

The Birthday Party

Saturday morning, the morning of Maddie's seventh birthday, dawned hot and bright, with not a cloud in the clear blue of the sky. I was in the kitchen blowing up balloons, and Jacqui, the mother of Maddie's best friend Chloe, had the party pies in the oven, paper plates and serviettes on the table and was icing cupcakes with a panache I couldn't hope to match.

Suddenly the back door was flung open and my wife stared around the kitchen, her eyes fierce. I recognised that look.

'Where have you been, Emma?' I asked. 'It's ten-thirty. The party starts in an hour and a half.'

Ignoring me she fixed on Jacqui. 'What do you think you're doing in my kitchen?' She was itching for a fight – I recognised the tone.

'Helping me prepare for the party,' I said mildly.

Emma stared at Jacqui, the deep lines on her face hardening. 'I know what's going on,' she said.

'Emma, don't be ridiculous!' I said. 'We're getting ready for Maddie's—'

'Oh Geoff, you think I don't know? You've been screwing her for years!'

Jacqui gaped at Emma, her face a mixture of shock and disbelief.

'That's rubbish and you know it,' I said. 'Jacqui, I'm sorry about this. Can you give us a few minutes? Or maybe go and get Chloe. We'll be fine now. Thanks so much for your help.'

'Are you sure?' Jacqui gave me a long searching look then turned and hurried out the front door.

There was a long heavy silence. For the first time we'd performed our tired old routine in public, and I realised our marriage had sunk to a new low. I was silent for a moment, wondering what to do. What mattered most was Maddie's party. An hour and a half before her little friends arrived: perfect timing, Emma.

'Where have you been all night?' I snapped, hoping she'd storm out before anyone else witnessed her in such a state.

Her face went rigid, her eyes like coals burning into me.

'None of your business!' she shouted.

Maddie came running into the room, her little face anxious. 'What's wrong?' she said.

Emma turned on her and screamed, 'Get out you stupid brat! I wish you'd never been born – you've ruined my life!'

Maddie stared at her mother, then burst into a storm of tears.

'Maddie sweetheart—' I began, reaching for her.

'Don't be pathetic! Grow up – stop crying,' Emma snapped. Then, when the child sobbed even harder, Emma turned and stormed out the back door. I could hear the metal caps of her shoes hammering the concrete steps, then the roar of the car as she sped away.

Maddie turned towards me. Her eyes were flooded and she was biting her lip, trying unsuccessfully to keep herself from crying. I scooped her into my arms, kissed her wet cheek and began to stroke her hair, murmuring to her until she began to quieten.

'I want you to try to forget what Mum said, okay? She didn't mean it. She's sick – she's not well right now,' I said, trying to soothe her.

Maddie sniffed. 'What's wrong?' she said, her soft heart touched.

'Nothing for you to worry about. Let's talk about it after your party. Your friends will be here soon.' I wiped her eyes and felt her body sag as the tension slowly drained out of it. 'Come on,' I said, 'let's wash that face and get you into your party dress.'

She gave me an uncertain smile.

By three o'clock that afternoon Maddie's friends had gone home and she and I were sitting at the kitchen table writing a thankyou list before we forgot who gave her each present. Paper plates with half-eaten party pies were strewn across the benchtop, serviettes and burst balloons lay crumpled on the floor and torn wrapping paper was scattered all over the living room.

I looked at Maddie. The excitement of the party had faded and although she seemed to have enjoyed it, she was quieter and more withdrawn than usual. Trying to comfort her, I reached across and caressed the back of her hand.

'When will Mum be back?' she asked, looking up at me.

'Did you enjoy the party?' I said, side-stepping the unanswerable question.

She nodded. Sunlight poured through the double glass doors and I gazed out at the back garden. Maddie's cubbyhouse stood in the back corner, partly hidden by jasmine, its fragrant flowers tumbling over the little door. It seemed like only yesterday that I'd built it for her. Maddie loved playing in it, arranging her tea set on the little table for her Barbies.

I knew that Emma and I had crossed a line that morning. Her attack on Maddie had ratcheted things to a new level. Her violent and volatile emotions I could deal with – had been dealing with for years – but Maddie was fragile and impressionable; I had to protect her at all costs.

'Why did Mummy say that to me?' Maddie asked, as if reading my thoughts. Tears brimmed in her eyes once more.

I sighed. 'It's the sickness, sweetheart. Mum needs to take her medicine so she'll be well again. Mum loves you. She loves both of us.'

'And you love Mum, don't you?' Maddie asked earnestly.

'Yes,' I said, 'I do. I've loved Mum since she was twenty and I was twenty-two.' I'd unconsciously slipped into storytelling mode and Maddie looked up at me expectantly.

'Tell me some more,' she said, resting her head on her hand.

'Well, we were students. I was at Melbourne uni studying engineering and she was at art school studying painting. We met at a party in Carlton. I thought she was so beautiful, she reminded me of a painting herself.'

Maddie stared at me, absently twisting a strand of hair around her finger. 'So you and Mum got married?'

'That's right. But first Mum and I went backpacking in Thailand. We got married in a Thai temple. Mum just decided. She was like that – a free spirit. Impulsive, I guess. I loved that about her.'

I felt Maddie's eyes on my face. After a while she said, 'When did Mum get sick?'

I felt my heart begin to pound and blood rush to my face. I'd always known we'd have to talk to Maddie about her mother's illness, but I'd hoped we might do it together. It seemed that would not be possible – it was finally time to talk to Maddie.

Taking a deep breath, I began. 'Maddie, Mum suffers from a mental illness. That means the sickness is in her head. You can't see it, but it's always there. It's called bi-polar disorder. Mum's had it since she was a very young woman.'

'But she doesn't look sick,' Maddie said.

'I know, but the sickness is there, in her head. There's medicine that keeps Mum healthy, but sometimes she stops taking it.'

I paused, looking at Maddie, trying to gauge her reaction, but her face was expressionless. Was that enough? Had I said too much?

'She said she wished I hadn't been born.'

'She didn't mean it. It's the sickness talking, not Mum. She loves you more than anything in the world.'

'When was I born?' Maddie asked.

'When we returned from Thailand. Mum got pregnant very quickly. Grandpa and Grandma Hart helped us buy a house ...' I hesitated. How much should I tell?

'And then I was born,' Maddie said with satisfaction.

'Yes, then you were born. But then Mum got very sick. She had to stay in hospital for a few weeks.'

'That's sad,' Maddie said. 'When did she begin to get better?'

'The doctors gave her medicine and she started to feel well again. But Mum doesn't like the medicine—'

'Does it taste bad?' Maddie asked sympathetically.

'Maybe. Mum says it makes her feel numb. So sometimes she stops taking it, and then she gets sick again.'

'Maybe it's my fault she's sick,' Maddie whispered.

'No sweetheart!' I said, grabbing her in a fierce hug. 'Mum was sick before you were born. She's just unlucky.' I gave her a quick squeeze. 'You were the best thing that ever happened to Mum, and to me. We were over the moon when you were born.'

Maddie was silent for a while. Eventually she looked up at me and said, 'I'm glad you told me, Dad. It helps me understand.'

'Do you feel a bit better now?'

She nodded, then slid off the chair and walked solemnly from the room.

That night I lay in bed staring up at the ceiling, hands clasped behind my head. Sleep eluded me, and I found myself thinking about Emma and our life together after the episode that hospitalised her after Maddie's birth. The darkness weighed heavily on me and the tapping of insects and whining of a solitary mosquito seemed loud in the night.

Like a movie reel, the years with Emma unspooled before my eyes, years punctuated by spells of wild creativity and joy, followed by ugly moods, harsh words and then periods of calm and contrition. I remembered the times when Emma would lock herself in her studio in the back garden, sometimes for days on end, immersed in her painting, refusing to sleep or eat. 'I'm not hungry,' she'd call over her shoulder when I brought her a snack. Or she'd chase me out, screeching at me for disturbing her. When finally she'd emerge from these euphoric spells of creativity, she'd party with friends until all hours of the morning, coming home disoriented and exhausted. At those times I wondered if she even remembered she had a daughter.

I'd been able to protect Maddie from the worst of it when she was a baby and toddler – she thought her mother was fun when she was in a manic phase – then Emma seemed to settle down once Maddie started kindergarten. These last few years had been good for all of us.

'It's lovely outside,' Emma would say, 'let's take Maddie to Luna Park.' We'd jostle our way through the crowd, throw table tennis balls into the mouths of clowns, listen to the roar of the rollercoaster and eat fairy floss on the ferris wheel.

But in recent months Emma had begun to skip her medication again, and I knew those carefree days of carnivals, sunshine and togetherness were under threat once more. It was as if I'd been holding my breath for years, waiting for a blow, and now it had fallen.

The following Sunday morning, I woke while it was still dark to the sound of the front door and footsteps on the floorboards. Emma had come home, at last. Still groggy from lack of sleep, I stumbled into the kitchen and found her standing at the sink filling the kettle. The top buttons of her blouse were undone and her hair was unkempt and dishevelled.

'Are you okay? Where have you been?' I asked.

'To hell and back.'

Her eyes looked flat and glassy, and I sensed that she was not aware of where she had been or what she had done. Seeing her so disorientated and vulnerable, my mood shifted from dread to compassion. 'Come here,' I said. 'Let me give you a hug.'

'I'm so tired,' she said as I embraced her.

'Sit down Emma. I'll get us a cup of tea.' Handing her a mug, I said gently, 'What's happened?'

'I don't know, I stopped taking my meds,' she said, looking down at her hands. 'I couldn't stand it – it's like being half-dead . . .'

'I thought so.'

'They make me feel so disconnected; like a different person. They anaesthetise me.'

'I know Emma. But look what happens when you go off them. Last time I had to rush you to hospital to get your stomach pumped. Remember? And what about Maddie? It was her birthday!'

'I know,' Emma said, her voice breaking. She wiped her eyes with the back of her hand. 'I can't believe I said those terrible things to her. I'm so sorry, I didn't mean . . .' She began to cry quietly.

'You may not mean it but you do real damage; you can't take back those words. Maddie is older now and she's much more aware of what's going on. She's much more sensitive to your moods. We need to protect her, Emma.'

She nodded miserably.

'How was the party?' she asked after a long silence. 'What happened after I left?'

'The party was okay, although I'm not sure how long Jacqui can be relied on to keep quiet.'

'Oh God,' Emma groaned, 'there goes my chance for a place on the Parents Club!'

I smiled. 'Afterwards Maddie asked me about your behaviour and I decided to talk to her about your illness. I think she's old enough to understand the truth. Better to know your mum's sick and doesn't know what she's saying, eh?'

Emma clasped her head in her hands, her fingers covering her ears. I didn't know whether she didn't want to hear or whether she was concerned for Maddie.

Lifting her head finally, she asked, 'How did she react? What did she say?'

'She felt sad for you,' I said. 'And I think she blames herself, despite my best efforts.' After a pause, I continued. 'Emma, this can't go on. Things have to change.'

She looked up sharply. 'Do you want me to leave?'

'No, Emma, of course I don't want you to leave – I love you.'

Her eyes filled with tears.

'But I want you to promise me that you will see your doctor regularly and book yourself into the Melbourne Clinic to get your meds reviewed. You need to get stabilised, and maybe there's something new, something better, so you won't feel half-dead all the time.'

'You know how much I hate that place, Geoff,' she said. 'My parents made me go there when I was a teenager – the locked doors, the relentless monitoring, it almost killed me.'

'I know it's hard for you Emma, and I'm not forcing you to do it. But if you want to keep our family together, you need to sort yourself out.'

I heard footsteps, and turning I saw Maddie standing uncertainly at the kitchen door.

'Come here honey and give me a hug,' Emma said, her voice wavering.

Maddie stood frozen for a long moment.

'I don't know what got into me,' Emma said. 'I know I said some horrible things, and I didn't mean a single one ...'

Maddie approached her mother and kissed her cheek.

'I hope you can forgive me,' Emma said.

Maddie nodded, burying her face in her mother's hair.

'I love you Mum but I don't like it when you're sick.'

'Yes, Dad and I have just spoken about that. I'll go to the doctor, and I'll do whatever I can to get well.' Her trembling voice was full of pain and regret.

She put her arm around Maddie. 'I promise I will not hurt either of you ever again,' she said, looking at each of us intently. She reached for my hand and I looked deep into her eyes. When she was like this, I could almost believe her.

Weekend at the Coast

When I saw her I stopped dead, coffee cup halfway to my lips. It was the first time I'd seen her in more than thirty years. Her body still moved with a youthful grace – those years on the athletics track at university had established a level of fitness that she had clearly maintained – and she was dressed elegantly in a silk blouse and cigarette pants. She looked every inch the successful business-woman – very different from the torn jeans or caftans she often wore when I'd known her.

As I watched her, something choked up in me. I remembered the mistake I'd made all those years ago and was overcome with a sense of loss and regret.

My instinctive reaction was to jump up, call her name and hurry over to speak with her, but I held back. She might not welcome my intrusion into her life – I had no idea what she'd done with herself since I'd known her, or who now shared her life. I gazed at her as she walked towards the cafe, feeling suddenly desolate as I thought of my own unhappy marriage.

I wasn't proud of the way I'd behaved when she and I had last met. I remembered our disastrous weekend at the coast all those years ago, when I'd made such a fool of myself. My face burned with embarrassment as I recalled my behaviour.

Nicky had called as I was sitting in the lounge room at home, a coffee in one hand and Keynes's General Theory of Employment, Interest and Money in the other.

'Josh, my parents have finally agreed to let me go to the coast.' I could hear the excitement in her voice. 'Can you come?'

Before I could make up an excuse, she went on, an imploring note in her voice, 'We can hire a cabin, walk on the sand, cook on an open fire … and we can be alone for once.'

As she spoke I felt all the energy drain from my limbs. Suddenly the safety of my routine life felt under threat. All at once I was certain that if Nicky got to know the real me she would despise me. How would we spend our time? What would we talk about? What if she suggested a bushwalk? I was not comfortable in the outdoors, and my mind filled with thoughts of leeches battening onto my ankles, snakes coiled behind every log, and branches just waiting to fall as I walked underneath – widow-makers they called them, didn't they? But then there was Nicky … I really wanted to be with her, so I decided to present a confident façade and hope that she didn't see through it.

'I'm going to take my easel and you can bring your books. It'll be fun. Please come,' she said.

'I'll see what I can do,' I said.

There was a long silence. 'Okay.'

The next day I rang her early. 'Let me get this straight. You're leaving on Saturday for ten days?'

'Yes. Can you come?'

'Well, I can't come for the whole ten days, but what if I come on Friday morning and stay until Monday. I've got a lot of study to get through, so I can't be away for too long. How does that suit you?'

After a beat she said, 'Okay I guess,' her voice flat.

'Right. Well, I have to go,' I said hurriedly, and put down the phone.

Early the following Friday I packed my car with all I'd need for the weekend: a cask of wine to help manage my anxiety, my book on Rothko to boost my artistic credentials and impress Nicky, but not my runners – without them I'd have a good reason to avoid bushwalking.

On the drive, I flipped between anxiety and excitement. Alone with Nicky ... but what would we talk about? As an introvert, I struggled to speak in company, and when I did, I preferred not to waste my time on small talk, but to speak instead about loftier issues such as the Vietnam War, Sartre or contemporary art. But did I really know enough about any of those topics to stand up to hours of conversation over several days? Suddenly seized by panic, I pulled over, wound down the window and sucked in several shuddering breaths. I don't think I can do this, I thought as I tried to calm my breathing. Of course you can. Think positive; think about being with Nicky, I told myself.

I drove on in such a storm of anxiety that I barely noticed the paddocks and rundown farmhouses, the flattened carcasses beside the road. Slowly the farmland gave way to dark, damp bush that looked somehow primordial and threatening. It began to rain. I saw glimpses of wild ocean and rocky headlands, all of it alien. Finally, I reached my destination, happy to see buildings, car parks, familiar signs of human activity. I took a deep breath and stepped out of the car.

Nicky always greeted me warmly and that day was no different. When I finally stopped outside her cabin she ran out and dragged me back in under the verandah, where she greeted me with hugs and kisses, then more hugs, more kisses. She held me for a moment then said, 'Hey, relax, Josh, what's wrong?'

'It's been a long drive,' I said, not meeting her eye.

She let me go and swept her arm around to take in the view. 'Isn't this a great place?' she said, indicating a parrot of some kind perched in a nearby tree.

'I brought some wine – let's have a glass,' I said, changing the subject before she could quiz me on my knowledge of native birds.

'Why?'

'We're on holidays.'

'Come inside, then. I've made sandwiches.'

'Sounds good.' I grabbed my backpack from the car and followed her into the cabin.

It was the first time I'd been to Wilson's Prom. The air bit at my cheeks and the park felt quietly hostile; the tall trees seemed to close in on me and I felt claustrophobic and unnerved.

I dropped my things on the bed.

'Leave it, Josh. We can sort out sleeping arrangements later,' Nicky said with a smile. 'Come and have a bite. The rain's eased.'

We stepped out onto the verandah and I noticed firewood stacked at one end. For a fleeting moment I imagined us in front of the open fire, naked, our limbs entwined. The thought reassured me as we sat side by side sipping claret and eating chicken sandwiches while I searched for something to say. I watched Nicky out of the corner of my eye and wondered whether I was punching above my weight.

Don't mess this up, I told myself. It was the first time we'd really been alone together – no one to disturb us, no one to invade our privacy and no other men to take her from me.

'How's the painting going? Are you happy with anything you've done so far?' I asked as I leant over and kissed her on the cheek.

She smiled and said, 'It's going well. I found a spot on the bank of the river. Each day I take my easel down and paint these huge rocks – they're like giant skulls, one balanced on the other and stained by rain and lichen. I'll show you after lunch.'

I smiled at her.

'Yesterday I climbed one of them, just to see if I could.'

'Sounds dangerous,' I said.

Ignoring my caution, she went on, 'Last night I got the shock of my life. A huge owl was perched right outside the cabin, looking down at me with huge eyes.'

'I'm here now,' I said gallantly, hoping she'd never realise that the real me was cowering just beneath my masculine facade.

After lunch, we strolled down the path towards the river. The undergrowth on either side was thick and damp. As I peered around, I tripped on a root, went down on one knee and hurriedly righted myself, hoping Nicky hadn't noticed. When we reached the river we took off our shoes and socks, rolled up our jeans and walked along the edge of the water. It felt icy at first, but as we meandered on, Nicky took my hand and I forgot my discomfort, gently caressing her palm with my thumb.

'Here's the spot I was telling you about. Aren't those rocks spectacular? And I love the way the sun shines through the clouds and casts shadows over the landscape. I'm experimenting with watercolour, but it's so tricky. You really need to know what you're doing. And I don't want to be too neat and tight, so I'm playing around a bit with washes, letting the colour bleed onto the wet paper.'

I recognised the rocks from paintings I'd seen on the table when I arrived. Nicky was right: the watercolour softened the image, giving it a damp, misty feel. 'Less is more,' she liked to say.

At sunset I prepared the barbecue and Nicky made a salad. As we sipped our claret we talked more easily. I sensed she liked me, and when I spoke she always listened with keen interest, her eyes never leaving my face. But I was relieved the day was almost over. I hadn't messed up, and I was starting to feel more confident, less concerned that Nicky was judging me, almost safe.

As the sun set I stoked the potbelly stove and we dragged two mattresses out of the bunkroom and set them side by side on the floor. I talked about Rothko, and his subtle use of colour, leading on from comments I'd made about Nicky's watercolours. He was my favourite artist – a Russian Jewish abstract expressionist who had killed himself in 1970. His moody, soulful paintings seemed to express my own inner darkness and turmoil.

'I admire his technique, and his use of colour, but I don't get his art,' Nicky said. 'It's too abstract. What do you like about it?'

'There's a depth to his work, a spiritual quality. You say less is more, well in Rothko's work that is definitely true. The colours draw you in and I sometimes imagine myself as part of the canvas. His paintings can depict ecstasy and tragedy – mostly tragedy I suspect. Did you know he committed suicide?' I paused. 'Didn't even leave a note.'

'Imagine how his family must've felt,' Nicky murmured, almost as though she were thinking aloud.

'He was troubled. Perhaps he felt completely alone in the world.'

'But it's wrong.'

Neither of us spoke for a time, then Nicky sighed and turned to me. 'Josh, tell me about your family; you never talk about them.' She looked at me searchingly. 'Do you have any siblings?'

'I had a brother.'

'Had – what happened?' she asked gently.

'What's there to say? He's dead.'

'That's awful, I'm so sorry. How old was he when he died?'

'Ten.'

'What happened?'

'A car accident.'

'Was he older than you?'

I stood up, ignoring her question. 'I need some air,' I said, and strode towards the door. By the time I reached the verandah my panic had increased. I had to make a conscious effort to breathe deeply to calm myself. As I thought about Peter, the accident, the ambulance and my mother's hysterical weeping, I fought back my own tears.

I remembered how my parents had shut down after he died: the silence at the dinner table; Dad slumped in front of the television, mindlessly watching commercials or shows as if there was no difference between them; Mum's refusal to get out of bed on weekends. Peter had been the apple of my parents' eye, and our family had revolved around him and his various sports. Now he was gone, I was left to fend for myself in the face of my parents' withdrawal.

Eventually, I got my breathing under control and, revived by a watery gust from the river, I went back inside.

I lay down beside Nicky and tried to hold her but she turned away.

'What's wrong?' I asked.

'Nothing,' she muttered.

'I don't believe you.'

'Why won't you share your feelings with me? Why are you shutting me out?' she said.

'Let it go, Nicky,' I said, as firmly as I could. 'Now is not the time.'

We finally fell asleep in the early hours of the morning, but I didn't sleep well, tossing restlessly on the thin foam mattress. The room seemed stifling and airless, and I felt confined, boxed-in, desperate to escape Nicky's forays into my private world. I woke at dawn, stuffed my things into my bag and left while she was still sleeping.

As I was driving back to Melbourne, the heavens opened. Hailstones pounded the car and the radio was overwhelmed with static. Frustrated, I turned it off and thought about the short time Nicky and I had spent together, trying to convince myself that there was something missing between us, that something just wasn't right. But despite my best efforts, I remembered her hugs and kisses, her warm, open, affectionate nature. Maybe there was something wrong with me. How could I not care for her, love her? Why couldn't I allow her to love me? Why was it all so hard?

I thought about all the nights when those feelings of loss enveloped me. I thought about my parents consumed by their son when he'd lived, and emotionally absent after his death. One inescapable realisation gnawed at me: Peter was the one they loved the most, or maybe he was the only one they loved. I remembered how uninterested my parents had been in my friends, my schoolwork, my progress. Once Peter died, it was as if nothing mattered to them anymore.

Would that emotional fault line mark my entire life, I wondered.

Nicky was coming home on Monday and although I was anxious to speak to her, to make things right, I decided to ring on Tuesday, allowing her a day to unpack and settle into her normal routine. Now that we were apart, I longed to hear her voice, and as soon as it was a reasonable time on Tuesday morning I rang her.

'How are you?'

'Why do you ask?'

'I'm sorry I bolted …'

'I don't get it, Josh. I thought we were having a good time. I'm not sure I can forgive you for this.'

The phone went dead.

Suddenly I saw my abrupt departure from Nicky's point of view, saw that it was selfish and inconsiderate. So consumed by fear had I been that I had not given any thought to how she must have felt to wake and find me gone.

I jumped into the car and drove to the local florist, grabbed a dozen red roses and sped to Nicky's house, hoping she would accept my peace offering.

'I am really sorry,' I said, handing her the flowers as she opened the door. 'Please forgive me, I messed up.'

Nicky looked at me guardedly. 'Thank you for the flowers,' she said.

'Is all forgiven?' I begged.

She hesitated, looking at me carefully. 'Why don't you trust me?'

Not knowing what to say I just stared at her.

'I know you care,' she said. 'I'll be here for you, but only if you'll talk to me.'

I swallowed, scared and confused. I don't know if I can do this, I thought.

'I really like you, Josh.'

Without thinking, I took Nicky's hands, looked into her eyes and kissed her softly on the lips. We held each other close and I felt a lump form in my throat. I clenched my jaw, trying to stop myself from crying, but it was too late. I could feel the tears rolling down my face. This was the one thing I'd dreaded, the one thing I had desperately tried to avoid. I was no longer the fun-loving, self-assured guy I pretended to be. What would Nicky think of this blubbering mess?

She pulled a tissue from her pocket and wiped my cheeks. 'I've never been fooled by that joker facade, Josh,' she said gently. 'I've always known you're sensitive – perhaps too sensitive sometimes.'

I felt ashamed. I was weak – an emotional wreck – and I didn't understand what she could possibly like about me.

That night I couldn't sleep. I sat at the kitchen table drinking coffee and eating chips, trying to hold back my tears. Why couldn't I be stronger? I was not worthy of her. And I was ugly – those lines on my forehead, the gap in my teeth, my nose, my hair – how could she even look at me? It would never work. She could never like the real me – my introverted personality, my social anxiety … what was there to like?

In the morning, feeling vulnerable and over-exposed, I decided to cut all ties with Nicky.

As I sat in the cafe, remembering that anxious and lonely twenty-year-old kid, I felt only sorrow. If I could have just told him not to be so afraid, reassured him that he was capable of love and worthy of being loved.

Having crossed the street, Nicky walked into the café and sat down by the window. Had she noticed me? Did she remember our time at the beach? Did she still remember the callous and inconsiderate way I had ended our relationship? I had thought about her a lot over the years and now, unexpectedly, here was my chance to show her that I had changed, that I was no longer the emotional wreck who'd hurt her all those years ago.

Ignoring my concerns about invading her privacy, I got up and tentatively approached her.

'Remember me?' I asked cautiously.

Nicky turned and looked at me warily. 'How could I forget? I wondered whether you would come and say hello.'

'Did you see me?' I ventured.

'Yes, I saw you. But given our past history I thought it best to leave you alone.'

'Can I join you?'

She hesitated. 'Okay,' she said, with slight reluctance.

'I've thought about you a lot over the years,' I said.

'Me too …' she replied, 'I mean I've thought about you.' She was looking at me, sizing me up.

'It's been a long time,' I said.

'Yes, over thirty years.'

'Much has happened since then. I like to think I'm a different person.'

She gave me a considering look, her expression questioning, curious. Then she said, 'Tell me about yourself.'

So I told her about my children – their careers, their partners and how proud I was of them – about my wife – her preoccupations and my loneliness in our marriage. I told her about my career, and how work had become a refuge from my unhappy home life. I was surprised at the ease with which I disclosed the intimate details of my life, and by the expression on Nicky's face; I could see she was surprised too.

'You have changed Josh. You're not so buttoned up.' Her face softened, the corners of her mouth lifted and her eyes seemed less guarded. 'I'm pleased for you,' she said warmly. 'You needed to; you were so inaccessible, so unhappy.'

I caught her eye, nodded and said, 'I think I've grown up, finally. And I've learned that when you're with someone, no matter how daunting it seems, you have to be daring, you have to risk being yourself, being open.'

Nicky smiled. 'Well, I'd better take your advice,' she said, and filled me in on the details of her life since last we'd met: her recent separation, her work as a designer, her current show at Gallery 52.

'Tell me about your ex,' I asked.

'There's not much to say. We split almost a year ago – it's over.'

'Why did you separate?'

'I admired him, respected and trusted him completely, which is why I think I was so shocked and upset when I discovered his infidelities. Now I just pity him.'

I shook my head slowly and said, 'I'm so sorry to hear you've had such a difficult time.'

She sat silent. Her eyes caught mine, held and then looked away. The silence between us grew as I tried to gather the courage to ask if I could see her again. I finally said, 'I'd love to see your work at Gallery 52. Could we arrange to meet there sometime – maybe next week?'

Nicky held my gaze for a long time. Then she said, 'I think I'd like that.'

Coming Out

'Can I talk to you, Mum?' Lucy said, hesitating at the door into the kitchen.

'Of course,' I said as I shut the fridge. For weeks Lucy had been withdrawn and moodily preoccupied. I'd left her alone until she was ready to talk, but lately the strained atmosphere had become intolerable. Now I hoped she was finally ready to share her problems with me.

'You look exhausted, darling,' I said as I turned and sat down. 'You're so pale and you've got dark circles under your eyes.'

'Thanks, Mum,' she said wryly. 'I didn't sleep most of the night.' She yawned and scratched her head.

'What's up?' I asked, part of me hoping that the discussion wouldn't take too long. Ian and I were meeting some of his colleagues for lunch, and he'd be back from the hardware store at any moment.

Lucy hesitated and said, 'I'm not sure you're ready to hear this, Mum . . .'

'Try me,' I said gently, glancing at the clock then back to my daughter.

She swallowed and fixed her gaze on me. Then she took a breath and said, 'Have you heard of transgender?'

I stared at her blankly.

'Do you know what it means?'

'Well, I . . .'

'Mum, I'm in the wrong body,' Lucy burst out, her eyes locked on mine. 'I'm not meant to be a girl.'

I felt my stomach clench and a wave of nausea overwhelmed me. After a moment I opened my mouth to speak, but I couldn't think what to say. I realised I didn't really know what transgender meant, or what Lucy was talking about. The silence lengthened, then I heard Ian's car pull into the driveway. Thank goodness, I thought disloyally.

'Lucy, I'm sorry. We need time to talk about this, but Dad's ready to leave,' I said.

Lucy sighed.

'I know it's terrible timing but we've made arrangements to meet some of Dad's colleagues in the city and we're already running late,' I finished lamely.

'Sure. Go, Mum; we'll talk about it later,' Lucy said, her voice flat.

I grabbed my bag, rushed out to the car, flung myself into the front seat and burst into tears.

'What's wrong?' Ian asked as he turned down the footy commentary.

'Drive, drive, and I'll tell you,' I said, fumbling for a handkerchief.

We drove down our ordinary suburban street, which no longer looked so ordinary.

'Lucy just told me she's . . . transgender,' I said through my tears.

He looked at me curiously for a moment, then turned his attention back to the road. 'That's this week,' he said flatly.

'I don't even really know what she means,' I said, hunting for my phone and tapping transgender into the search bar. After a moment I read out, 'Relating to someone whose identity and gender differ from their assigned sex at birth.' I felt my throat tighten.

Ian was silent, his jaw set. He listened as I continued to search, reading out snippets about bullying, medical intervention, hormone therapy, surgery, suicide . . .

Lunch was strained, and afterwards I sobbed all the way home, finally able to express the emotions I'd been forced to suppress.

As a family, we had enough to contend with, I thought, awash with self-pity, and now this! I needed a knee replacement and Ian's job was precarious. Life was already hard enough. But most of all I felt as though Lucy – the beautiful girl I'd birthed and nurtured – was taking herself away from me. It felt like theft. Memories of her as a toddler, a little girl, a teenager, scrolled through my mind, and I grieved for every one of them. Lucy had shattered everything.

As soon as I opened the front door I saw her sitting in the living room. She glanced up, startled, her eyes following her father as he stalked down the hall and into his study. We both heard him shut the door firmly.

Watching her, I allowed myself for the first time to think that Lucy's jeans, t-shirt and sneakers might signify something more than merely the uniform of youth. Her hair, brutally short around the ears and flopping over her forehead, now looked like a military cut.

'Hi, how are you going?' I asked. Sunlight streamed through the wide expanse of glass onto the carpet and a breeze lifted the blind. 'I'm so sorry we had to rush off on you like that.'

'I'm okay,' she said quietly.

'Lucy, how long have you felt this way?' I asked as I sat down on the couch opposite her.

She hesitated a moment and said, 'I've always felt different, Mum – wrong somehow. But I didn't want to think about it. Then I saw a show on TV six months ago about a teenager living as a transgender person. I couldn't hide from it anymore . . . suddenly everything made sense.'

I shook my head, trying to think clearly. 'You found out by watching a TV show? Lucy, are you sure—'

'No, Mum, you don't understand. That's when I stopped lying to myself. I recognised myself in that kid. We'd had the same experiences.'

'I'm so confused,' I said. 'Tell me, if you don't mind my asking, are you attracted to men or women now?'

She screwed up her mouth and gave a sardonic little grin. 'You know I could never be with a guy,' she said, her voice slightly hoarse.

This was no surprise. Lucy had come out as gay when she was thirteen. I'd thought that was enough to cope with.

'Do you intend to have a sex change?' I asked, startled to hear the words come out of my mouth.

'Yes, I think so, Mum. Eventually. There's a lot to consider . . .' She stared at her hands.

Suddenly, I had a vision of her body, scarred and mutilated, that beautiful little body I'd nurtured and cared for over so many years. I was flooded with panic at the idea of it – the countless surgical procedures, the piles of medical bills, her suffering. I reached over, took her hand and said gently, 'Lucy, can't you be happy with just dressing like a boy?'

She sat bolt upright, looking at me in shock and indignation. 'No! Mum, I'm not a girl. I'm in the wrong body. When I take off my clothes I'll still be in the wrong body. I was meant to be a boy!'

I lay in bed that night looking blankly at the Bergner painting of twisted pots and pans on the wall. Ian was undressing in the walk-in robe. 'You don't seem to be very upset by all this,' I remarked.

'I'm not,' he said as he hung up his suit.

'Why not?' I asked. 'I'm so frightened . . .'

He looked at me, rubbed the side of his face and said, 'It's transient, Caro, it'll pass.'

I stared at him as cold dread moved through me. Ian was not going to travel this difficult road with me; I was on my own. His denial left me feeling utterly abandoned.

'How can you be so dismissive?' I asked, sitting up and leaning against the bedhead. 'I really don't think this is a passing phase. We need to support each other through this, and support Lucy.'

'Okay, you just wait and see,' he said as he got into bed. 'It's a fad, a stupid teenage fad she's picked up from her lesbian mates.'

I was exhausted. There was no point talking to him further. I turned to face the wall, closed my eyes and tried to sleep.

Lucy was in the kitchen squeezing orange juice when I came in the next morning. She turned to face me, her eyes heavy and dull.

'Can I make you a juice, Mum? You look exhausted,' she said as I sat down at the kitchen table. She regarded me carefully, concern etched on her face.

The sweet cool juice felt like a salve to my parched throat. 'Lucy, I think you should go and see a psychiatrist.'

'What?' She narrowed her eyes. 'I'm not sick, Mum. Why do you say that?'

'Well, you've got a long and difficult road ahead. There're going to be lots of bumps to negotiate and I think you'll need some professional support . . .'

Lucy's shoulders twitched and a shudder moved through her thin frame. She sighed. 'Yes, you're right, Mum.' She sat down next to me and grabbed my hand. 'Will you come with me?' she asked, her voice tight with fear.

'Of course,' I said, and squeezed her hand. 'We're in this together.'

A few minutes after Lucy had left for school, Ian came into the kitchen.

'How did you sleep?' I asked.

'Fine,' he said, taking down a plate and dropping two slices of bread into the toaster. He avoided looking at me.

'Just so you know,' I said, 'I've spoken with Lucy and she's agreed to see a psychiatrist.'

'You're wasting your time and our money,' he said, glancing at me. 'By next week this will all be over.'

'You're in denial, Ian!' I snapped. 'She's our daughter, I'm not taking any risks.'

He shrugged and said, 'Do what you like, Caro.'

It was my rostered day off, fortunately, and once Ian had left for work, I sat on in the kitchen, my head pounding. Had I done something to cause Lucy's gender confusion? Was all this somehow my fault? Was it because I'd called her Louis when she cut her hair short and refused to wear dresses? Was it because I teased her about being a tomboy? Why was she rejecting her womanhood? I called our local doctor and made an appointment for the next day.

The following afternoon, we walked into Dr Naidu's rooms.

When Lucy explained that she was transgender, Dr Naidu gave her an encouraging, sympathetic smile. She'd been our family GP since Lucy was a baby and she knew her well. She asked Lucy a series of questions and when I requested a referral to a psychiatrist she leaned forward, placed a hand on Lucy's shoulder and said, 'Your mum's right, Lucy. A psychiatrist will guide you through some of the challenges of gender reassignment.' Then she added, 'Dr Bowden specialises in this area. He's very good. I'll write a referral for you to see him immediately.' She glanced at me and smiled.

'Thank you,' I said, and we stood up to leave.

When we arrived home I immediately dialled the number and took the first available appointment – a cancellation.

Lucy asked me to go with her, so four days later we drove to East Melbourne to the specialist's rooms. The receptionist ushered Lucy into the consulting room but I was taken aback when she directed me to remain in the waiting room. As Lucy's mother, shouldn't I be included?

For an hour I flicked mindlessly through women's magazines, wishing I could eavesdrop on the conversation. I still couldn't believe I'd been left excluded. Eventually, the receptionist approached and told me the doctor would like to see me. About time, I thought.

I walked in to see Lucy wiping tears from her eyes.

'Lucy, darling, are you okay?' I asked, alarmed.

'Hello Mrs Morrell,' Dr Bowden said. 'It's good to meet you.'

I collected myself. 'Thank you, Dr Bowden. Now please fill me in on what you and Lucy have been discussing.'

He looked at me benignly. 'Lucy and I have had a long chat. We've agreed that she'll come and see me weekly.'

'Weekly?' I said. 'Is that really necessary?'

'Yes, Mrs Morrell, it is necessary,' he said firmly. 'Lucy needs to be guided through the transition process.' He paused momentarily. 'Furthermore, gender reassignment will be life-changing for her as well as the family, so you and Mr Morrell will also need support. I recommend you also see a psychiatrist.'

I stared at him and swallowed hard. He was very authoritative and didn't seem to invite discussion or debate. After a long silence I asked, 'Okay, Doctor, who do you recommend?'

He was quiet for a moment. 'Let me think about who might be appropriate.'

We walked in silence to the car, but before I started the engine I turned to Lucy. 'So how did it go, darling? Are you okay?'

She stared at me and tried to say something, but the words would not come out. She cleared her throat. Then, in a choked voice she said, 'Mum, I'm really scared.'

I felt my heart surging and the blood beating inside my head. It had finally sunk in that this was real. It was actually happening, and I wondered whether I had the capacity to support Lucy through this. It felt as if my world was crumbling around me.

'I'll be here for you every step of the way,' I said, not really sure I could keep my promise.

She shifted uneasily in her seat and ran a trembling hand through her hair. She had the look of a frightened, hunted animal.

'It's during the difficult times in our lives that we learn most about ourselves,' I said. 'It's when we grow.' This sounded like a platitude even to me, but I was trying to reassure her. She nodded mutely.

I turned on the ignition and drove out of the carpark, a lump the size of a cane toad in my throat.

'I'm sorry, Mum. I'm sorry to put you and Dad through this,' Lucy said as we turned onto Victoria Street, which was bathed in soft autumn light.

'Don't be silly.' I patted her knee. 'You were born this way honey – it's not your fault. It's nobody's fault.'

At dinner that night Ian and I were alone. Lucy had gone out with some friends, and I was relieved to see that she seemed a little less anxious. Ian avoided my gaze and his energy was flinty and aggressive. Finally, he looked at me and said a little belligerently, 'So, how was your session with this Dr Bowden then?'

I hesitated. 'He said Lucy doesn't need to be medicated and they agreed she would see him weekly. He also recommended that you and I see a psychiatrist.'

'What for?' he said, slamming his knife and fork down on the table.

It was exactly the response I'd anticipated. I sighed heavily. 'Dr Bowden says gender reassignment is not only life-changing for Lucy but also for us, and we'll need support.'

'That sounds like psycho-babble to me,' Ian retorted. 'I'm not going.'

I just looked at him, overwhelmed with fatigue. Finally I said, 'I don't accept that, Ian. I've made an appointment for next week and you're coming. Lucy is your daughter and you can't absent yourself from this.'

Ian's face contorted with indignation and he stood up from the table, taking his plate to the kitchen.

'I'm really tired,' I said as I followed him out and placed my plate on the sink. 'I'm going to bed. I'll leave you to stack the dishwasher.'

The following Wednesday Ian and I walked into Dr Schwartz's consulting rooms.

She stood as we entered and gestured for us to sit down. 'How can I help you?' she began.

I cleared my throat nervously and said, 'Our daughter, Lucy, has come out as transgender and her doctor suggested we seek guidance from a psychiatrist.'

She was silent for a long moment, looking at me, then at Ian and back to me.

'And how do you feel about that?' she said in a soft voice.

I burst into tears. All the stress of the past few days gathered into a storm front and I could no longer control my emotions.

Eventually I wiped my eyes, cleared my throat and said, 'I feel like Lucy is dying and I can't do anything about it – I feel helpless.' My fingers tightened around my handkerchief and I could feel my lips trembling.

Dr Schwartz turned to face Ian. 'And what are your thoughts about this, Ian?'

'It'll pass,' Ian said curtly.

Dr Schwartz seemed taken aback. 'Can you elaborate on that?'

Ian hesitated for a moment, then his nostrils flared and he said, 'No, I can't.' It was obvious that he had no intention of engaging any further with Dr Schwartz.

I felt ashamed of my husband. 'What's behind all this?' I said, uncomfortable with the lengthening silence. 'Is it something we did or didn't do?'

Dr Schwartz glanced in Ian's direction, then turned back to me. 'That's a common question,' she said. 'Rest assured, there's nothing you've done that has made Lucy transgender. It's who he is.'

Ian sat stolidly silent while we spent the rest of the consultation discussing my concerns about Lucy.

At the end of the session Ian and I walked silently to the car. We didn't speak about the consultation at all and after a few days of this awkward impasse I realised we hadn't spoken much about anything. The tension in the house was palpable. Ian became more aloof and withdrawn and spent most of his time alone in his study. He no longer cooked, cleaned or participated in the life of the family. Our marriage seemed to be falling apart.

One Friday night, as we sat together watching television, Ian exploded. 'It's your fault, Caro!'

'What's my fault? What are you talking about?' I said, shocked.

'All this!' he said, gesturing wildly. 'Lucy . . . this whole transgender rubbish . . .'

I looked at him, aghast.

'You're just encouraging her, giving her your blessing to continue down this ridiculous path.' His eyes were wild with fear and rage. 'I just can't comprehend why anyone would want to change their gender!' he continued, pacing across the room. 'It's freakish. It can only end in disaster. Look at the trouble it's already caused – our family is falling apart! And I don't know who she is anymore. I'm ashamed of my own daughter.'

I wanted to run from the room. His words felt like an assault on Lucy, and on me. Finally, I was able to collect myself and in a tremulous voice I said, 'Ian, try to understand. She's a boy in a girl's body.'

'I've never heard anything more absurd!' he roared. 'This must stop!' He marched from the room, leaving me bewildered and alone.

Three weeks later I was admitted to hospital for a knee replacement. After the operation I had a severe allergic reaction to the medication and for four days only close family could visit. At one stage the doctors were concerned that I might not pull through.

On the fifth day Ian and Lucy came to see me in the ward. Although they had been by my bedside for the last five days in the intensive care unit, only now could I open my eyes and look at them, even croak a few words in an attempt at conversation.

As soon as they walked through the door I sensed there had been a shift in their relationship. Ian looked calmer and Lucy was walking tall for the first time in what seemed like years. She was less defensive somehow, more at ease in her body.

'How are you feeling, Mum?' Lucy asked as she took my hand.

'I'm doing okay,' I croaked. 'I saw the doctor this morning and she's happy with my progress.'

Ian smiled at me kindly.

'So, how are you two managing?' I asked, eyeing them curiously. My anxious predictions of open warfare seemed not to have materialised.

'Actually Caro, we're doing well,' Ian said as he glanced at Lucy.

'I thought so,' I said. 'Tell me what's been going on.'

'We've had a lot of time together and it's given us an opportunity to talk,' Ian said. He perched on the end of the bed.

'You gave us a fright, Mum,' Lucy said. 'It kind of put things in perspective. You know, about what really matters.'

'What kind of things?' I asked nervously.

'The essentials,' Ian said.

'He means the people we love,' Lucy said with a grin, and they exchanged a glance. Something had definitely shifted between them over the last few days.

'We've talked a lot,' Ian said huskily, then cleared his throat.

'And I think I'm beginning to understand Lucy and the whole situation a bit better.'

'Go on,' I said.

'Well, as it turns out, one of my colleagues, John, has a daughter who transitioned, and I've been talking to him about it all.' He looked down at his hands. 'It's been . . . helpful.'

I decided not to press him further. Ian had re-joined the family, and in his no-nonsense way he was putting the past weeks firmly behind him. Lucy and I exchanged a look that said it all.

A few days later I was sitting on the edge of the hospital bed, my legs dangling over the side, when Lucy poked her head around the door.

'Good morning,' she said warmly. 'You've got more colour in your face today, Mum.'

I smiled faintly, then said, 'I feel a bit sore, but I'm okay. I'm so heartened by the shift between you and Dad. Frankly, it's the best medicine anyone could give me.'

Lucy grinned. 'Last night I told Dad that I've changed my name to Louis.'

I gasped, shocked that the daughter I had named could shed that name so easily. But I reminded myself that this was part of the long and challenging journey we were all travelling. And at least Louis was a pet name we'd used before.

I took a sip of water and asked tentatively, 'How did he respond?'

'It took him a moment or two to get his head around it,' Louis said. 'Look, I know this is really difficult for him and that he's struggling, but a lot of things changed when you were sick. Dad and I talked and talked. Partly it helped us cope with our fears that you might . . . you know, and maybe once he'd faced one fear it was easier to face the others. He's been incredibly brave and supportive. Anyway, after a while he accepted my new name – even practised using it a bit.'

I took a deep breath. 'Let's go for a walk to the courtyard for some fresh air.'

'Are you sure?'

'Yes, the physio told me I have to exercise the muscles that support the knee.' I stood up gingerly and Louis passed me my crutches. We made our way slowly down the corridor and through the double doors into the courtyard, with its round tables and birch trees.

I flopped onto a bench with a sigh of relief and Louis took my hand. 'I'm sorry for the trouble I've caused you and Dad.'

I looked my child in the eye and said, 'Lucy . . . Louis, I am so proud of you, of your courage . . . and for being true to yourself and living your life with honesty and integrity. As my daughter you always made me proud and I have no doubt you will make me equally proud as my son.'

Louis's eyes filled with tears as he took my hand and we watched the morning sunlight dance across the leaves.

The Thief

Bob sat in the pub, breathing in the stale air that filled the dim room. John, who had parked himself opposite, noted idly that the lines on his mate's face looked deeper and his sandy-coloured hair was uncombed. Above him hung a fading Cezanne print, yellowed with cigarette smoke.

Together they watched Harry collect a jug of beer from the bar and make his way back across the cracked vinyl, around the shabby tables and chairs, to where they were sitting.

'Thanks mate,' John said as Harry filled his glass.

'Next round's mine,' Bob said, ashing his cigarette and gulping down half his beer.

Bob, Harry and John had been meeting at this Melbourne hotel every Wednesday for the past six months, a ritual they rarely missed, and then only for a very good reason. Bob hadn't been able to make it for months, so this was a sort of reunion. Harry and John hadn't liked to ask what was up – they assumed Bob was working a case. Mostly they talked football and horse-racing – rarely anything intimate or personal.

Bob reached for an old Penthouse magazine on the sideboard, opened it to the centrefold and then tossed it aside. He sculled the rest of his beer and slammed the empty glass on the table.

'Hey, what's bugging you today, mate?' John said.

Bob shrugged, then busied himself rolling up the rumpled sleeves of his flannel shirt. 'That bastard Frank Romano just stole my wife,' he spat, dark eyes burning. 'My wife, the thieving mongrel.' He glared at the two men, jammed his cigarette in the ashtray then immediately lit another one. 'Gave her the best years of my life; gave her everything – never refused her. And then she bloody gets up and leaves!'

'Mate, what happened? Your wife left you?!' Harry asked, his round cheerful face etched with concern.

'Ran off with Frank Romano – we were all at school together,' Bob snapped.

'When did this happen?'

'Last week. She packed her suitcase and just walked out.'

John, who'd been gazing out at the overgrown garden, turned towards Bob and fixed him with keen brown eyes. His glasses had slipped down the bridge of his bony nose and he pushed them up impatiently. 'So what did you do to deserve that?' he asked.

'Wha'd'ya mean what did I do! Not a bloody thing!' Bob said, raising his voice.

John's eyes narrowed. 'Mate, you must have done something.'

After a long pause, Bob grunted, 'I've had back problems.'

The two men looked at each other, nonplussed.

'Listen, I couldn't work,' Bob continued. 'Couldn't do a bloody thing. Two days a week I went to hospital for rehab and the rest of the time I was at home, stuck on the couch watching TV. It was bloody demoralising. Not that my wife cared,' he added bitterly.

'So that's where you were. We figured you were busy on a case.'

'Hardly. Stuck on my arse all day,' Bob grunted. 'And the worse of it is,' he added, 'she's turned the kids against me!'

'Hang on, mate, that doesn't make sense,' John said. 'Your kids are in their twenties. Surely they've got minds of their own.'

Pinching his cigarette between trembling fingers, Bob said, 'Listen, mate, whose side are you on? I'm the victim here. It wasn't me that ran off with someone else!'

'How'd you hurt your back?' Harry interrupted, attempting to steer the conversation away from conflict.

'I wrecked it during a drug bust and got pensioned out of the police force. That's when it started. Don't do this! Don't do that! It drove me nuts.'

'Back pain's horrific,' Harry said.

'Tell me about it. And sympathy? Forget it.'

'How d'you manage the pain?' Harry asked.

'Well, I guess I drank a bit ...' Bob said. 'But I'm not an alcoholic – like she said I was.'

Noting that the jug was empty, John picked it up and meandered up to the bar for a refill. When he returned, Bob and Harry were still talking about Bob's back.

'Did rehab help?' Harry asked.

'At first I hated it, but things eventually got better.'

'Yeah?' John finished filling their glass and said, 'Why, what happened?'

'I met Joan,' Bob said. 'She was in therapy, too.'

'Tell us more,' Harry said, his eyes lighting up. 'What's she like?'

'Well, it was more than good looks, though she's a looker all right. She understood me ...' Bob said. 'She cared.'

'So did you, you know, start a relationship with her?' Harry asked.

'Put it this way, we were more than just friends,' Bob said, grinning broadly.

John fixed his gaze on Bob and asked, 'And did your wife know what was going on?'

'Being the suspicious type she figured it out pretty bloody quickly,' Bob muttered.

'So what happened then?' John asked.

'My wife told me she was fed up with me. Moved into the second bedroom! Said she'd had enough of my boozing and whoring.' Bob took a long draught of beer. 'She blamed me. It never occurred to her that if she'd come up with the goods, I wouldn't've had to go looking elsewhere.'

Harry shook his head. 'They just don't get it, do they? And then they get pissed off when things don't work out the way they want ...'

'Then she got herself a computer,' Bob continued. 'Locked herself in her room. Well, any idiot could work out what that was about.' He ground his cigarette into the ashtray. 'I knew she was involved with another guy, so I got an old friend from the force to follow her,' Bob said, his cheeks flushed.

'And sure enough, I was right. Can you believe she hooked up with that arrogant son of a bitch, Frank Romano?' Bob slammed his hand down on the table. 'He and I were at school together; he was always such a smarmy turd. Thought he was better than everyone.'

'Bloody hell, you poor bastard!' Harry said.

'One night I confronted her – showed her photos me mate had taken of her and Frank.'

'Good likeness,' she said, 'the bitch. I told her she was never to see him again.'

'Fair enough,' Harry said.

'I knew I couldn't trust her so I never left her alone; I even went shopping with her. She whinged about it, but I wasn't interested. I reminded her that she was my wife!'

John leaned back in his chair, folded his arms and regarded Bob steadily.

'With my bad back, her job was to look after me, not take up with someone else. Whatever happened to "in sickness and in health"? She seemed to have forgotten that.'

John nodded, prompting Bob to continue.

'And then, just last week, she packed her suitcase and walked out the door. Said she wasn't coming back.'

John stood abruptly, his chair scraping harshly on the floor. 'Going for a leak,' he said.

Once inside, he leaned on the sink, waiting for his breathing to settle. He felt sorry for his mate – it couldn't be easy having your wife walk out on you – but this was as much Bob's fault as his wife's, John thought, staring into the mirror. He'd been selfish and inconsiderate, and now he seemed to believe he was entirely blameless. John heaved himself upright, pissed in the urinal, washed his hands and went back to the table.

'Listen Bob, I've been thinking,' John said carefully. 'Do you think maybe you're both responsible for this bust-up? I mean, your wife couldn't have been happy when you took up with Joan …'

'What the fuck?!' Bob exploded. 'She walked out on me!' His eyes shifted minutely and suddenly his face turned beetroot-red.

'Hey! That's him!' he roared. 'That's the bastard who stole my wife!' He thrust a trembling finger at a tall, broad-shouldered man in his late fifties. Jumping up, Bob sent his chair sprawling and pushed between the men watching the football on the bar TV. John and Harry hurried after him.

'You arsehole Frank Romano! You fucking arsehole!' Bob shouted.

Frank was sitting alone at the bar and looked around, startled, but before he could speak Bob threw a punch at him.

'Steady mate.' Harry and John pulled him off and hung on to his arms.

Frank reeled back. 'What's the matter with you? Are you mad?' His face pale, he glared at Bob and said through gritted teeth, 'When we left school I hoped it would be the last I'd ever see of you, you low-life scumbag.'

The pub fell suddenly quiet.

'Come on, mate.' Harry stepped in between Bob and Frank.

'He's crazy,' Frank said, shaking his head in disbelief.

'Are you all right?' John asked Frank.

'Yeah, he missed – like he always did. He's pathetic.'

They dragged Bob back to the table and pressed him into his chair.

'Stay put, mate, or you'll be up on an assault charge. You know that,' John said.

Bob's eyes burned as he stared at Frank. 'That bastard,' he muttered. Then a torrent of abuse began to pour from his mouth, his voice rising with each word.

Frank got up from his stool and strode over to the table. Fixing his eyes on him, he said, 'No wonder she walked out on you. What did you expect, you stupid prick? That's what happens when you hit a woman.'

John's eyes widened and he looked at Bob. Harry glanced up sharply.

'Well, she deserved it,' Bob said defiantly. 'She never looked after me; she needed to be brought into line!'

'You hit her?' Harry said in disbelief.

'Are you deaf?' Bob yelled. 'I said, she deserved it. That's the only language women understand.'

'You really believe that, don't you?' John said.

'You're damn right I do,' Bob spat at him.

Frank hadn't finished. 'My father knew your old man, knew what a violent brute he was, what he did to your mother,' he said. 'Seems like history's repeating itself.'

Suddenly Bob's eyes went flat and glassy. 'Leave my parents out of it,' he mumbled.

Frank gave him a look of pure contempt, turned and walked back to the bar.

John looked over at Harry. 'Let's go, mate. I've had a gutful.'

Being Here

Sarah was studying for her university exams, but she needed a break. 'Come for a walk,' I said.

'Dad . . .'

'Come on, you'll feel fresher after a bit of exercise.'

Ten minutes into the walk it began to rain.

'Dad, why don't you ever talk about the past?' Sarah said as we sheltered under a tree.

'What's brought this on?' I asked.

'I'm studying for my Indigenous Cultures and Histories exam. It's all about the past and how it affects the future. And it occurred to me that I know nothing about my own history.'

The veins in my temple began to throb. I saw afresh the stricken expression on my father's face when anyone mentioned the Holocaust.

'I'd love to go to Poland one day, to see where our family came from,' Sarah continued.

I took a deep breath and said, 'Sarah, your papa made me promise never to set foot in that country. As far as he was concerned, the Poles were as guilty of murder as the Nazis.'

'Well, Dad, I never promised and I really want to go.'

A cold anguish moved through me. Not knowing how to respond, I said nothing.

'I know that you and Papa never spoke about the past, and that it was a source of great tension between you. But don't you think it's time to find out about our history?' Sarah said, looking at me carefully.

'I'm not sure I can do that, Sarah,' I said, starting to feel uncomfortable under her scrutiny.

'But why?' she pressed. 'Why do you feel the need to keep our family history locked away, unacknowledged?'

'Well, to be honest, I'm scared of being sucked into a very dark world. My father was submerged in the past and he always seemed to be depressed. He had a very pessimistic view of humanity. I don't want to be pulled down into that. I have to protect myself.' I peered up at the sky. The rain had stopped.

'Look, Dad,' Sarah said as we walked back to the house, 'I understand. I get it. But maybe if you confronted the past you'd understand it better; it might even feel less threatening to you. Sometimes it's better to face up to the things we're afraid of, rather than running away from them. Don't you think it might be empowering to stare them down, rather than allow them to continue to frighten us?' She looked at me kindly, her face grave. 'Dad, I can see that you don't want to talk about what happened to Papa and our family, but I can also see that it weighs heavily on you.'

'What do you mean? How?' I said, immediately defensive.

'Dad . . . come on. The headaches, the ediginess . . .' She kicked at a pile of autumn leaves.

I glanced at her: my perceptive daughter. I'd never been able to hide anything from her.

That night I went to bed early and turned my face to the wall, but I lay awake for hours. Deborah rested a hand on my shoulder but I pretended to be asleep, and she turned away with a sigh.

It felt as if I'd only just drifted off when the blackness woke me – I felt it upon me, oppressive and ominous. I lay in bed, staring into the darkness, then closed my eyes and recalled my conversation with Sarah. I knew she was right: suppressing the painful memories of my childhood was exhausting. I was anxious and short-tempered, and I was afraid. All the time, I was afraid.

'You look pale Maurice. Are you okay?' Deborah said as I came into the kitchen.

'I slept badly,' I grunted.

'I know, you were very restless. What's bothering you?'

I slumped into a kitchen chair. 'Yesterday, Sarah and I went for a walk and she told me she wants to go to Poland. She asked me if I'd go with her.'

'Wow,' Deborah said, exhaling, 'that must have brought up a lot for you.' She came to the table and sat opposite me. 'What did you say?'

'I told her the thought of going to Poland terrifies me and that I promised my father I would never set foot in the place.'

'And how did she take that?' Deborah asked as she buttered her toast.

'Well, she reckons the reason for my headaches and anxiety is because I haven't dealt with my family history . . .' I watched her carefully to gauge her reaction.

Deborah gave me a sympathetic look. 'You know, Maurice, I think you should go. It's about time you faced all that. You and I both know it's been eating you up for years.'

I couldn't deny she was right; but the very thought of Poland twisted my stomach into knots. 'If we decide to go, Deb, will you come with us?'

She paused for a moment before saying, 'No, I think it's important that the two of you go together.' She took my hand and said, 'It's not my heritage.'

I walked to the window and stared into the street, seeing neither the trees nor the traffic. Instead, I saw my father on a different street. It was a Sunday morning and he was sitting at a café table on the footpath in Brunswick Street with two men. As I approached them, I heard snippets of their conversation: 'What happened to your family during the war?' one man asked my father.

Dad stiffened and looked away, then he turned to face his companion and was about to speak when he noticed me standing by their table. Startled, he clamped his lips shut.

At that moment, I understood the barrier that had always stood between my father and me. His refusal to talk to me about what had happened to his family during the war had created an immeasurable gulf between us. It had made intimacy and trust impossible.

At dinner that night I was subdued. Sarah kept glancing at me throughout the meal. At one point, she put down her soup spoon and said, 'Dad, I'm going to go to Poland whether you come with me or not. But it would mean so much to me if you'd come. And I think it would be really good for you.'

Once again, the pain of growing up in a Holocaust-haunted house flooded into me. I recalled my father sitting at the wooden table on the back veranda, staring blankly into the branches of the silky oak. I so wanted to know what he was thinking about, but I knew never to ask.

I took a deep breath. 'Sarah, I've been thinking about our conversation, but the thought of going to Poland horrifies me.'

Deborah interjected, 'If you go, I could meet you in Prague at the end of your trip . . .'

'And I could go to Berlin to meet a couple of my friends,' Sarah said.

Deborah continued, 'A few days together in Prague will give you something to look forward to after the challenges of Poland.'

Sarah reached for my hand across the table. 'Dad, I don't want us to have the same troubled relationship as you had with Papa,' she said.

I swallowed hard. 'What do you mean? Don't we have a good relationship?'

'Well, we do,' Sarah said, withdrawing her hand, 'but you are very guarded. And I'm always a bit afraid of provoking your temper.'

She was right again. I couldn't deny it.

Deborah raised her eyebrows questioningly.

'I need to think about it,' I said with a sigh. 'It really is a huge thing for me. Give me some time.'

I sat on the plane gazing at the clouds. Below us was Poland. A graveyard.

'Fasten your seatbelts for landing,' the flight attendant said, puncturing my dark ruminations. I took a deep breath, reaching for some calm.

Sarah turned to me and for a moment her clear dark eyes gazed directly into mine.

I heard my father's voice: 'Promise me you will never set foot in that fuckin' country, Maurice!' Yet here I was. I felt drained and hollow at the thought that I was betraying him. Yet a part of me acknowledged that I was trying to create something different and good between my daughter and myself – a relationship that was open and honest. I wanted to ensure that history didn't repeat itself.

Sitting in the back of the taxi on our way to the hotel, I turned towards Sarah and said, 'Do you want to hear the weirdest thing? When I stepped onto the airport tarmac, I had the uncanny feeling that I had come home.' The awareness had left me so shocked and bewildered that it had taken me this long to even articulate it.

Sarah looked at me, her expression thoughtful. 'Well, when you think about it, it's not that surprising. I mean, you are only a first-generation Australian, after all. Our family roots go back much deeper into Poland than they do into Australia.'

I had never thought about it that way, but she was right of course. Nevertheless, it was very disconcerting. I was a tourist in this city; I had never been to Warsaw and all my life I'd been indoctrinated into its horrors, yet it felt weirdly familiar to me.

Once we had checked in to the hotel we walked around the old town square, past the Royal Castle, into the Saxon gardens. Feeling suddenly hungry, we stopped at a café. From its open doors wafted the comforting and familiar smell of what I always thought of as 'Jewish food': chicken soup, schnitzel, pierogi. Immediately, a happy lightness settled on my chest.

We walked in and, glancing around, I saw plates laden with dishes that reminded me of my childhood: gefilte fish, challah with chopped liver, kreplach soup.

As we sat down at a rickety wooden table, I looked at Sarah and said, 'I want you to know how wonderful it is to be here with you.'

Sarah's eyes widened and she smiled. 'I can't tell you how happy I am to hear you say that, Dad,' she said.

The following morning after breakfast, Sarah and I went downstairs to reception where we met Jerzy, our tour guide. A man in his late fifties, he had straight white hair, a short beard and tortoiseshell glasses. I was surprised to note he was wearing a beige fishing vest over his short-sleeved check shirt.

As we walked across the road he asked, 'Where would you like to go today?'

'Please take us to my father's family home,' I said. 'It's at 66 Zelazna.'

'Of course.' We climbed into the car. 'On the way we can stop at the wall of the Warsaw ghetto.'

As we wound our way through the back streets of Warsaw, Jerzy said, 'You know it was the biggest ghetto in the territories occupied by the Nazis? In 1942 alone they sent 254,000 Jews from the ghetto to Treblinka extermination camp in a matter of months.'

I swallowed hard and took a deep breath as we arrived at the ghetto wall and stepped out of the car. Standing in front of the memorial plaque, I felt my eyes prickle with tears. I took another deep breath. After a few moments, I was finally able to breathe without difficulty, but the heaviness in my chest remained. I thought about my paternal grandmother who, while breaching ghetto curfew one night, was murdered by the Nazis. I felt a strong urge to run from this place, but at the same time I felt compelled to stay, to bear witness and to honour all those who'd died.

Sarah noticed my tears and looked up at me in surprise; I had never cried in front of her. She stepped towards me and put her hand on my shoulder.

Back in the car, we drove past unkempt buildings, their concrete facades still riddled with bullet holes in places. Stray cats scrambled through garbage bins and the footpaths were strewn with old newspapers and rubbish.

We arrived at a four-storey building with tarnished white-framed windows and graffiti on its brick façade. From the paved inner courtyard, I looked up at the apartment on the first floor where my father had lived as a boy. A man was standing on the balcony.

'Can we come in?' Jerzy said in Polish.

'Wait a minute,' the man said as he turned to go inside.

Returning a few minutes later, he looked down at Jerzy and said, 'My wife said to tell you it's not convenient. We have visitors.'

I had a sudden vision of that man during the war years – storming Jewish homes, throwing occupants onto the street and stealing property.

Overhearing our conversation, a neighbour, a woman who looked to be in her eighties, asked us, 'Where do you come from?'

I was surprised that she spoke English.

'Australia,' I replied. 'My father lived in that apartment before the war,' I said, pointing.

'Come up,' she said. 'I'll make you coffee.'

I turned to look at Sarah, then Jerzy; both nodded.

We walked up the stained stone steps that echoed with the shouts of children who were racing up and down the stairs and sliding down the banisters.

'I know the apartment where your father lived,' the old woman said as we walked through her door.

I nodded, encouraging her to continue.

'I've lived here all my life and I knew your father's family.'

There was a long silence as I tried to absorb the enormity of this.

'Do you know what happened to them?' I was finally able to say.

She looked at me, hesitated a moment and said, 'One night the Nazis came with their dogs. They broke down the door of their apartment while the family was sleeping and threw them out onto the street.'

'Not an uncommon story,' Jerzy remarked.

'Later that day, my parents arranged for my uncle to hide them in the basement of his house in the country,' the woman told us.

Peering closely at her, I asked, 'Do you remember anything specifically about the family?'

'Well, I'm an old lady, it's hard for me to remember details. But I think the young boys were twins. One of them played the violin, if I remember correctly . . .' she said. 'I seem to recall that his name was Ephraim.'

I felt goose-bumps and began to shake. 'That was my father's twin brother,' I said, my voice trembling.

I felt Sarah stiffen next to me. 'Do you know what happened to Ephraim?' she asked.

'I'll never forget that day,' the woman said, sighing deeply. 'I was visiting my uncle in the country when a Nazi patrol car sped up the long driveway. They must have been tipped off. I was standing at an upstairs window; Ephraim was playing outside.'

The woman paused, seeming to gather herself, before continuing. 'The Nazis screeched to a stop out the front of the farmhouse and three of them got out of the car, moving towards him. They spoke to the boy for a moment then, holding him tight, they pulled down his pants to see if he was circumcised. And then they shot him.'

Sarah gasped and put her hands over her mouth. I was immediately overwhelmed by a mountainous rage. My father's tormented expression on those winter nights flashed before me; those moments when he sat staring out at the garden, seeing neither the silky oak nor the garden beds. Now, I clearly understood why he refused to ever return to Poland, why he carried so much unspoken pain.

At dinner that night Sarah picked up a bread roll from the cane basket in the centre of the table and I saw a tear drop to her cheek.

'What's the matter?' I asked.

'I was thinking about Ephraim.'

'It's a horrible story.'

'An innocent little boy with his whole life ahead of him.'

'And only one of countless horrible stories from the Holocaust.'

'War is a terrible thing.'

'Let's not dwell on that,' I said, deliberately trying to change the subject.

'I guess there's nothing to be gained,' Sarah said, forcing a smile. Then she added, 'Dad, I really appreciate your coming with me on this trip. It's meant so much to me, thank you.'

'It hasn't been easy, but it's been . . . very worthwhile,' I said, tearing off a piece of roll.

Placing her knife on her plate she said, 'It's actually been life-changing for me, Dad. It's helped me clarify what I want to do with my life.'

'Oh? Tell me more?' I said, raising an eyebrow.

'I've decided to work with Indigenous people,' Sarah said.

I looked at her curiously, then nodded for her to continue.

'Well, in some ways, Jews and Indigenous people are quite similar,' she said. 'The Nazis stole land from the Jews and white colonists stole land from the Indigenous people.'

Leaning forward she continued, 'And the Nazis tried to wipe out the Jews while white Australians tried to, at the very least, breed out the Indigenous people.'

'Yes, I can see the parallels,' I said, heartened by Sarah's sensitivity and intelligence.

After a moment's reflection, I continued. 'You know, it's been life-changing for me, too. It's been cathartic.'

Sarah smiled warmly and encouraged me to elaborate.

'Being here has helped me understand the depth of my father's pain. It's helped me to forgive him for being so . . . absent.'

Sarah took my hand and smiled.

As we walked back to our hotel after the meal, I placed a hand on my daughter's shoulder. I felt that together, we were writing a new family story.

Acknowledgements

I was privileged to have the assistance of many people while writing these stories, which would not have been possible without the help of Nadine Davidoff. I learned a remarkable amount about writing from her. She has been a source of great insight and guidance and I owe her a huge debt of gratitude for her incredibly generous support. I am truly grateful to her. She gave willingly of her time and I have benefited from her understanding, acumen and direction.

I am grateful for the help of Nan McNab. Her extensive work in editing these stories has been instrumental in making them infinitely better. I have greatly benefited from her insights, counsel and assistance. She has been remarkably patient with me, nothing was too difficult, and she was a pleasure to work with.

My heartfelt thanks to Bob Sessions for his support and guidance in the publication process. I have also benefited from the endless hours of typing and retyping by Noni Carr-Howard. Sam and Diana Seoud set aside a table at their café, Dundas and Faussett, to enable me to write.

Finally, many friends have been there for me along this journey. They are too numerous to name – you know who you are. Thank you for your support and encouragement. And last but not least, thank you to my family for your enthusiastic support and helping me keep everything in perspective.

Bernard Marin AM was born in 1950 and graduated from the Prahran College of Advanced Education in Melbourne in 1970. He established his accounting practice in 1981 and currently works with the staff and partners of the practice as a consultant. Bernard has held a number of positions on various boards, including: Treasurer – Melbourne Writers Festival (2005–16), Koorie Heritage Trust (2000–08), and Liberty Victoria (de facto, 1984–92); board member – Australian Centre for Jewish Civilisation (2009–15), Reichstein Foundation (2011–12), Melbourne Community Foundation (2009–10), and Koorie Heritage Trust (2000–12).

Bernard is the author of *Selection in Human Resource Accounting* (1982); a memoir, *My Father, My Father* (Scribe, 2002); *Good as Gold: A Novel* (Harvard Publications, 2017); and *Stories of Profit and Loss* (Harvard Publications, 2019). Bernard lives in Melbourne with his wife, Wendy.

www.ingramcontent.com/pod-product-compliance
Lightning Source LLC
Chambersburg PA
CBHW021433110726
47901CB00008B/2411